SABOTAGE

Blood Ritual:
The Adventures of Scarlet and Bradshaw, Volume 1
BY THEODORE ROSCOE

Champion of Lost Causes
BY MAX BRAND

The City of Stolen Lives: The Adventures
of Peter the Brazen, Volume 1
BY LORING BRENT

The Complete Cabalistic Cases of Semi Dual,
the Occult Detector, Volume 2: 1912–13
BY J.U. GIESY AND JUNIUS B. SMITH

Doan and Carstairs: Their Complete Cases
BY NORBERT DAVIS

The King Who Came Back
BY FRED MacISAAC

The Radio Gun-Runners
BY RALPH MILNE FARLEY

The Scarlet Blade: The Rakehelly Adventures of
Cleve and d'Entreville, Volume 1
BY MURRAY R. MONTGOMERY

South of Fifty-Three
BY JACK BECHDOLT

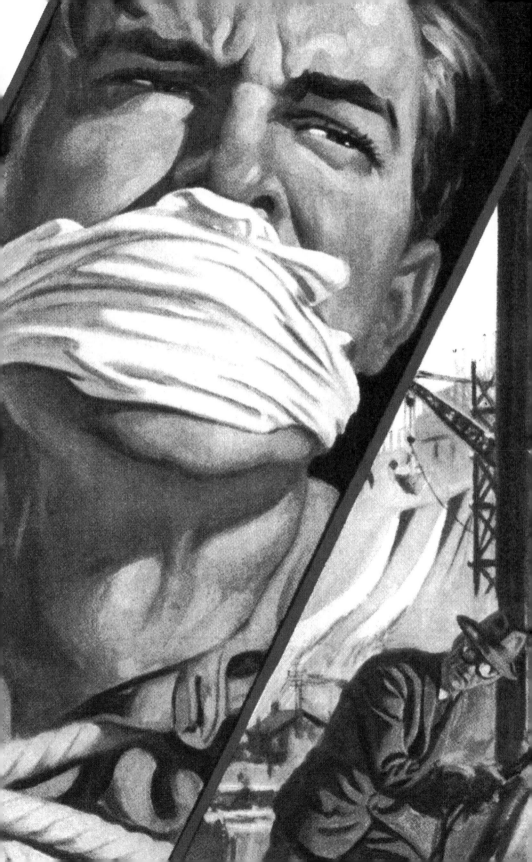

SABOTAGE

CLEVE F. ADAMS

COVER BY

EMMETT WATSON

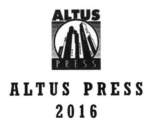

ALTUS PRESS

2016

© 2016 Steeger Properties, LLC, under license to Altus Press • First Edition—2016

EDITED AND DESIGNED BY
Matthew Moring

PUBLISHING HISTORY
"Sabotage" originally appeared in the March 11, 18 and 25, and April 1 and 8, 1939
  issues of *Detective Fiction Weekly* magazine (Vol. 126, No. 5–Vol. 127, No. 3).
  Copyright © 1939 by The Frank A. Munsey Company. Copyright renewed ©
  1966 and assigned to Steeger Properties, LLC. All rights reserved.
"About the Author" originally appeared as "Motivation in Mystery Fiction" in the
  May 1942 issue of *The Writer* magazine (Vol. 55, No. 5).

THANKS TO
Chad Calkins, Everard P. Digges LaTouche and Evan Lewis

ISBN
978-1-61827-226-3

Visit *altuspress.com* for more books like this.
Printed in the United States of America.

TABLE OF CONTENTS

CHAPTER I

TO GET YOUR THROAT CUT

THE DIRECTORS' TABLE was of mahogany, polished till it shone like a mirror. Before each of the assembled men lay the customary blotter, the usual fountain pen set and the pad of blank forms. But these were arranged about the edges of the long table. The center was bare. Reflected in the softly glowing wood, as in a pool, were the faces of the men themselves, symmetrical as eggs in a carton. The dozen faces, McBride thought, were a little like eggs at that, and, carrying the illusion still further, he was reminded of the old saw about putting all your eggs in one basket. That, indeed, seemed to be the predicament in which these twelve gentlemen found themselves. They were members of the Alliance of Pacific-Southwest Underwriters and their individual companies had been taking a terrific beating on the Palos Verde Dam project.

McBride was not at the table. Even had he been a director of the Alliance he was not by nature a sitter. He stood with his back to the tall windows, careless and a bit arrogant before the financial wizards who had called him in. He looked like a million dollars. He was stony broke.

The chairman of the group cleared his throat. "Your record is not too good, McBride."

"I'm not trying to sell you anything," McBride said. "You sent for me."

There was a subdued murmur at the table. There was scarcely a man here for whom McBride hadn't worked. Any one of

them would have been glad to have him back, yet collectively they were afraid of him. Perhaps they themselves were appalled at what they expected him to do.

The chairman coughed gently. "I mentioned your record, McBride, because this matter is a trifle more important than recovering stolen jewels or proving a life claim fraudulent. You get results, I'll give you that, but your methods are not always"— he appeared slightly embarrassed—"always too tactful. You are known as a gambler and apparently you have an unholy attraction for women. I merely wish to remind you that whoever is behind the sabotage of Palos Verde will advantage themselves through your weaknesses."

"I didn't know they were weaknesses," McBride said. He picked up his hat and topcoat from the chair at his side. The topcoat was an imported camel's-hair for which he had paid two hundred dollars. He wondered what it would bring in a hock shop. He said, "Well, it's been nice seeing you all again."

There was a hurried shuffling of chairs. The third man from the end on the left hand side stood up violently. He was a roundish, roly-poly little man with thinning sandy hair and high blood pressure. His name was Rourke and he was vice president of Acme Indemnity.

He said:

*"I'll need five grand expense
money," said McBride.*

"Now wait a minute, McBride."

He evidently expected McBride to wait because he immediately turned his back on him and addressed the chairman. "Damn it all, Charles, we sent for McBride because we needed him; because everything else we've tried hasn't worked. What do we care if he's an out-and-out lecher? What do we care if he's the wooden Indian he looks like? Are we hiring a detective or a Sunday school teacher?"

Franz Charles permitted himself a bleak smile. He was very tall, taller even than McBride, though not so heavy. The smile was no more bleak than the rest of him. He could have been carved from gray granite. He said, "Even the government puts some restrictions on its men."

Rourke pounded the table in an access of rage. He said, "A hell of a fine comparison that is, but it proves my point. They've sent government men to Palos Verde, haven't they?"

Charles shrugged. "Whatever the majority wants is all right with me."

McBride said, "Don't mind me, gentlemen. Just discuss my private life as though I weren't here. And when you get all through you can ask me if I'll take your lousy job. There's always that to consider, you know."

Rourke pointed a dramatic finger at Charles. "See what you've done? You've antagonized him, that's what!"

Charles put his cold eyes on McBride. "Palos Verde is the biggest government contract ever let. The dam will be the largest in the world. Leeds & Leeds got the job. We're underwriting Leeds & Leeds. Do you understand that?"

McBride said he did. He said, "You forgot to mention that Palos Verde is only the first of these super power projects. What Leeds & Leeds does on this one will probably determine the acceptability of their bid on the next."

The cold eyes warmed a trifle. "You knew we were going to hire you, didn't you, McBride? You even looked up some of the answers in the back of the book, didn't you?"

McBride studied his nails. "Maybe."

Rourke banged on the table. "Didn't I tell you he was smart? Didn't I?"

Nobody paid the slightest attention to him. Charles said, "Between us our coverage includes employer's liability, work-men's compensation, damage to machinery, delay due to strikes, acts of God, any and everything. In other words, if Leeds & Leeds are sunk, we are sunk too, only we'll be sunk first. We're getting ours already. Every time a worker gets himself killed it costs us ten thousand dollars. Every time a mixer jams it costs us more. We've paid out close to half a million dollars in the last ninety days. Think you can stop it?"

"I don't know," McBride said.

"Ever hear of the Five Companies?"

"Theirs was the losing bid."

"Does that give you any ideas, McBride?"

"Maybe."

Rourke banged the table loudly. "You don't have to tell McBride his business, Charles. He knows what he's going up against. He knew before he came here. He knows that Leeds & Leeds have hired dicks, and that we have hired dicks, and that the damned accidents still go on. What's the use of hag-gling?"

Charles looked at McBride. "Do you think I'm haggling?"

"Not over money," McBride said. "I've never kicked on what any of you paid me. I just didn't like some of the jobs, is all. They smelled." He got a certain sardonic satisfaction out of the uncomfortable silence which followed. Served 'em right for the cracks about him. He said, "I'll need some expense money."

EVERYBODY looked relieved. Even the austere Mr. Franz Charles, though only his eyes showed this. He pressed a button below the edge of the table and presently one of the secretaries came in. McBride's eyes glowed warmly as she passed him. Though he couldn't identify the perfume she wore he thought he would recognize it again should he ever meet it in a dark room.

Charles said, "Make out a check, Miss Ford." He lifted an eyebrow at McBride, and McBride said, "Five grand will be enough now. I'll probably need more later."

Miss Ford said, "A check for five thousand to Mr. McBride. What initials, please?"

"Just Rex," McBride said. "And yours?" She colored faintly under his stare. At the table behind her someone seemed to be having trouble with his breathing. It was Rourke. He shook his head at McBride, who was gallantly opening the door for Miss Ford. Charles was openly displeased. He said, "You might at least have waited till you got outside, Mr. McBride."

"It was in here that you gave me the reputation," McBride said. He went out, banging the door behind him.

Miss Ford was running the check through the protectograph. She was still flushed. McBride said, "I'm sorry I was rude in there. They'd just got through making me out a heel. Maybe I am."

She looked at him. "It's of no consequence."

"Meaning you're still sore? Tell you what I'll do—I'll go back inside with you and apologize in front of the whole works."

"That isn't necessary, Mr. McBride." She carried the check into the directors' room. McBride, shrugging into his topcoat, looked at the three other girls in the outer office. Not one of them was worth a second glance. He went over to the ash blonde at the reception desk. "What's Miss Ford's first name, sister?"

"I don't think she'd—" The blonde met McBride's warmly admiring glance. "Well, don't tell her I told you, but it's Kay." She returned abruptly and guiltily to her typing as the inner door opened and Miss Ford came out.

McBride accepted the check, stuffed it carelessly in a side pocket. "Thank you very much, Miss Ford."

She nodded stiffly. He put on his hat and went out of the office and down the corridor to the elevators. He thought that he had never seen eyes as darkly blue as those of Miss Kay Ford. He wished he didn't have this perverse streak that made him notice things like that, because he was very much in love with someone else. He cashed the check at the bank downstairs. He discovered that he was a little drunk with the sudden possession of all that money after a very bad week's run at the crap table in the back room at Louie's. To sober up he crossed the street and went into Fiorello's bar. Palos Verde, Nevada, began to seem like a long way to go to get your throat cut.

CHAPTER II

FROM THE HOUSETOPS

THE CAB DRIVER said irritably, "Hey, which one o' these places you live in?"

McBride opened his eyes and saw that he was indeed in front of the bungalow court in which he lived. He knew it was the right court because nowhere else in Hollywood had he ever seen such a remarkably active fountain. It was practically impossible to reach one's front door without a mild shower. Colored lights set in the rim of the basin made a rainbow effect of the spray from the center plume. It was quite dark.

McBride ran a fuzzy tongue over parched lips. "What time is it?"

"Seven o'clock."

"Ummm. Any idea where you picked me up?"

"Sure. You come out of Louie's place and tells me I should drive you around a while. I been doin' this for a hour now, but I'm getting hungry, so I look in your pockets and find out where you live."

McBride sat up a little straighter. "You looked in my pockets?"

"Sure."

McBride, remembering suddenly that earlier in the day he had had the important sum of five thousand dollars, decided that he too would look in his pockets. He was startled to find that he now had slightly better than nine thousand dollars. This seemed to indicate that he had taken Louie or one of the house men for approximately four grand. He had no recollection of it. He rubbed the back of his neck and regarded the hacker with frank admiration. "You mean you actually frisked me and didn't touch the dough?"

"It is very bad business," the hacker said, "to roll a dick. Even a private dick. Besides," he added, "you might have remembered."

McBride selected a century, creased it thoughtfully and extended it. "The reward of honesty," he said. "Even such cautious honesty as yours." He got out of the cab. "I live in 4-B." He steered the driver carefully down the flagged walk so that he himself would be protected from the fountain. In 4-A, the other half of the double bungalow, a woman screamed shrilly and there was the sharply brittle sound of breaking glass.

McBride let himself in with a slightly unsteady key. "Good night, pal."

"Good night," the hacker said. He went off up the flagged walk, trying to skirt the fountain to avoid a wetting. He couldn't make it. Nobody could. McBride closed the door and went into the bathroom.

After a while the telephone rang. McBride came out of the bathroom naked and answered it. "Hello?"

"This is Kay Ford, Mr. McBride."

"Oh, how are you, Miss Ford?"

"I just wanted to thank you for the flowers. They're lovely."

He looked blank. "Oh?"

There was a slight hesitation at the other end. Then, "Really, you needn't have apologized again, Mr. McBride. I wasn't so very angry with you."

"Well," he said helplessly, "well, you know how it is."

Evidently she expected him to say something else, but he couldn't think of anything adequate to say. He must have sent a card with the flowers. Anybody who could win four grand from Louie and not remember it was capable of anything.

Her voice drifted to him slightly tinged with something that might have been disappointment. "Well, thanks again, Mr. McBride."

"Sure," he said. "Sure." He replaced the phone and went back to the bathroom and stood under the needle shower for ten minutes. He felt fine.

Dressing, he regarded his reflection in the mirror. What was it Rourke had said? Oh yes, he looked like a wooden Indian. Well, he did kind of look like an Indian, at that. He wondered if any of his Black Irish ancestors had married Indians. Possibly they hadn't married them. Anybody who couldn't remember the last three or four hours certainly couldn't be expected to remember whom his ancestors had or had not married. He gave this up and began packing a bag. The telephone rang.

IT WAS Sheila Mason. McBride's mouth lost its sardonic twist and became curiously gentle. "Yes, Sheila?"

"I hear you saw the Alliance, Rex."

His face was suddenly wooden and his dark eyes became watchful, cagy. "Who told you that?"

"Aren't you forgetting that I'm on the legal staff of Leeds & Leeds?"

He had forgotten it. Always, when thinking of Sheila, it was a little difficult to remember she was an attorney. He said, "Excuse it, hon. I just had the idea that the fewer people knew about the job the better. The Alliance ought to know that."

There was a little silence at the other end. Finally: "You were going away without telling me, Rex?"

He made a bitter mouth. "What good would it do? Would you offer to go with me? Would you even give me a half promise that it would be worth my while to come back?" He laughed nastily. "A guy can't go on hoping forever, you know."

Her voice sounded tight, strained. "We've been over this so many times, Rex. I'm fond of you, you know that. Perhaps I love you. But Kenneth's death is too recent, the memory of my life with him—" She broke off, adding rather desperately: "I made one mistake, Rex. I don't want to make another."

He thought of her husband, and of something Franz Charles had said about him, McBride. Charles had called McBride's penchant for women and gambling weaknesses. Come to think of it, Ken Mason had been a little too fond of these. Among other things they had caused his untimely end.

McBride pushed this thought out of his mind. "Have dinner with me?"

"I've had dinner, Rex. I have to work tonight. I'm at the office now."

"All right," he said savagely. "I'm surprised you bothered to call up."

She caught her breath at that. "You're being a little unfair, Rex. After all, I'm on the inside of this thing. I—I know what happened to some of the other investigators. I merely wanted to ask you to be careful."

"For your sake?"

"Perhaps. Yes, if you like, for my sake. And for your own, Rex. Getting yourself killed won't solve anything for either of us." She hesitated. "Good night, Rex."

"And you won't have dinner with me?"

"Mr. Leeds is waiting for me. You're taking the night train out?"

Again his eyes got that cagy look. "Yes, eleven o'clock." He deliberately broke the connection. Then, knowing himself for a heel, he looked up a number in the phone book and dialed it.

"Hello, Miss Ford? Rex McBride. Would you have dinner with me?"

Her voice was pleasantly surprised. "Of course. Is this to be another apology?"

"No," he said, "I'm a little sick of apologizing for the way I live. This is a straight dinner engagement. I'll call for you at eight."

"I'll expect you," she said. "Until eight, then."

He hung up, stood there for a moment glowering at the

phone. He hauled a flat steamer trunk out of the closet and began packing in earnest. The last thing he put into the trunk beside a spare gun was a thick sheaf of currency. He held out less than a thousand dollars. Once more he picked up the phone, this time to call a cab, and when the cab came he gave the driver the trunk with instructions to express it collect through to Palos Verde. "Mail the receipt to Rex McBride at the Grand National."

The guy hauled the trunk out. McBride then called the airport and made a reservation in the name of John Smith for the eleven o'clock plane east. Hat and topcoat on, he snapped his bag shut, looked around the apartment as though he might not see it again, looked at his flat little .25 automatic as though he'd like to use it on himself, finally dropped it in a side pocket and turned out the lights. He let himself out the back door, so as to avoid the fountain in the patio, walked over to the boulevard and caught a cab. He thought that probably he was being an ass. On the other hand he might be a very great detective.

IT WAS five minutes after eight when he rang Kay Ford's doorbell. She wore midnight blue, and this, under artificial light, made her blue eyes seem darker than ever. She was older than she had been at the office, softer but somehow more poised. This time she didn't flush under McBride's admiring eyes. She said, "Do come in, Mr. McBride. I'll have to find my wrap. Would you care for a drink?"

He moved inside, closing the hall door and leaning his back against it. "Thanks, no." His eyes appraised the apartment. "Live here alone, Kay?"

"Yes."

"Nice place," he said. "Secretaries must make more money than detectives."

Her eyes laughed at him. "Now you *are* being a detective, aren't you? Am I under suspicion?"

"I suspect you of being a very smart gal," he said. His teeth shone whitely against the darkness of his skin. "You keep the card I sent with the flowers?"

"Meaning you don't remember sending them?"

He grinned. "You do pin a guy down, don't you?"

She sighed. "Well, it's something to know you remembered me, if you don't remember the flowers." She turned carelessly toward a communicating door. "The card's over on the liquor cabinet." She disappeared through the door.

McBride went over and looked at the card. It was one of his, all right. The penned apology and signature were his.

Miss Ford came out. She had changed to a street ensemble of some woolly gray material and she carried a gray camel's-hair topcoat. He said, "I guess I'll have to apologize again. I'm going away or I'd have worn a dinner jacket. You needn't have changed. Nobody in Hollywood cares what you wear."

She tucked a small hand beneath his arm. "Shall we go?"

They went out and down to the waiting cab.

It was a Friday night, and Julienne's, even at nine o'clock, was crowded with a lot of guys and dames who liked to miss all but the main event at the Legion Stadium. In other words, important people. You knew they were important because they looked important, and they spoke carelessly of how they had told off Louis B. Mayer. " 'Louie,' I says—" The food was good, though.

Waiting for a table, McBride and Miss Ford were at the bar, and McBride had just gotten down to the point where he was telling her that of all women he preferred those with black hair and violet-blue eyes. In a general sense this was quite true, especially the business about the black hair. The fact that Sheila Mason ran to gray eyes and coppery hair was beside the point.

Both McBride and Miss Ford were equally surprised when accosted by the executive vice president of Acme Indemnity. Rourke was in tails and his high blood pressure showed in his congested eyes. In the background hovered a girl who was not Mrs. Rourke.

"Damn it, McBride, I thought you were on your way to Palos Verde!"

"Have you told the papers yet?" McBride said. "Or the radio?" He took the little gun out of his pocket, proffered it. "If you want me killed off there's no sense waiting. Why not do it here?"

Rourke peered around him like an arch conspirator. His voice became a whisper. "Well—uh—well, you left the office at two. I thought surely—"

McBride bent his head gravely. "I'm taking the eleven o'clock train. Go away, will you?"

Rourke looked at Miss Ford. "I hope you know what you're doing, young lady."

She gave him a brilliant smile. "Oh, quite." Her eyes rested fleetingly on the lady in the background who was not Mrs. Rourke. "And you?"

Rourke backed away hastily. "We'll expect to hear from you, McBride."

"You won't," McBride said. Turning, he leaned on the bar and confided to his reflection in the mirror that he was supposed to be a detective, but that it was very difficult indeed, because so many other people knew it too.

Miss Ford said, "So you're going to Palos Verde!"

He frowned at her. "See what I mean? Now you know it. I don't know why we couldn't make a triumphal parade out of the thing."

She toasted him with her glass. "McBride comes to Palos Verde." Then, eyes like dark pools: "You're not serious about being killed?"

"Of course not," he said. "It's one of those things that can only happen once. A guy would be silly to take it seriously." Over the heads of the crowd he caught Julienne's signal and they went into the supper room. The orchestra was playing *Blue Hawaii*, and McBride, remembering this as one of Sheila's favorites, flushed dully. Then they were at their table, ordering.

He ate well. That was one thing about McBride. No matter

how depressed he was, an aperitif invariably served its purpose. He watched Miss Ford watch him. By and by he noticed that she wasn't eating. "What's the matter, hon?"

"I—I'm not hungry."

"You'd already had dinner," he said accusingly.

"Well—"

He said, "That's what I call being a good sport!"

"No, it isn't that. I—I just remembered something." She leaned toward him, blue eyes probing his darker ones. "You're in love with someone, aren't you, Rex?"

"Like hell I am. Unless maybe it's you, kitten."

She shook her head. "Unh-unh. I guess a woman sort of senses these things, Rex McBride. You called someone else before you called me. She turned you down." McBride paid the check and they rose to go. "I'll ride down to the station with you, Rex," she said.

"All right." They got in the cab. Neither said anything till they were bowling east on First Street and the terminal was only minutes away. He said, "I wish I could take you with me, Kay."

"I wish I could go, Rex." The perfume of her was like heady wine in his nostrils. He wanted to kiss her. He fully intended to kiss her, but somehow he didn't. When the cab drew up under the great glass and steel marquee all McBride did was shove a fist at her chin in rough good-fellowship. "Well, I'll be seeing you, kitten."

"Good night, McBride."

A redcap grabbed his bag and McBride had to chase him all the way through the rotunda to get it back. He went out the side entrance to the auxiliary cab rank and caught a hack for the airport. He very nearly missed the eleven o'clock plane. He was glad he hadn't, because the stewardess looked very interesting.

CHAPTER III

MURDER BY MISTAKE

THEY WERE HIGH over San Bernardino, perhaps seven or eight thousand feet up in order to clear the peaks, when McBride first noticed the gray man. He was that inconspicuous. It is no trick at all to go unremarked in a crowd, but to escape more than a casual glance in the narrow confines of a transport plane is to achieve real anonymity.

McBride was in Seat 7, the gray man two seats forward. McBride had passed him, coming in, but he was rather breathless from the run for the plane, and during the takeoff and the ensuing ten or fifteen minutes in the air he had been busy admiring the stewardess and the way she handled the blonde who was going to Palos Verde for a divorce.

Beyond the blonde was an old lady in black who alternately read from a limp-leather Bible and closed her eyes as though she might be praying. An empty seat intervened between the old lady and a red-faced, paunchy guy who couldn't be anything but a traveling salesman. The salesman was very indignant because the stewardess had told him he couldn't nurse the bottle he had brought along to ward off possible airsickness. He was telling the white-haired woman across the aisle how indignant he was. The white-haired woman could have been a dowager queen or the hostess in a honky-tonk. She wore a mink coat that must have cost thousands and there were diamonds on three of the fingers of her left hand. She let the salesman know

15

that his troubles were none of hers and buried herself in a morning paper.

Directly in front of McBride was a man so thick and wide that he bulged under and over his chair arm. Rolls of fat overlaid his collar and pushed his ears up against his hat brim. He had refused to be relieved of the hat. His skin had the peculiar dead whiteness of a fish's belly.

Gradually McBride became conscious that between the lady with the diamonds and the mountain of flesh immediately before him there must exist a sixth passenger. Seated, he couldn't see this man; he just somehow knew he was there. Presently he stood up, yawning, and went forward as though confused about the location of the lavatory. Reminded of his mistake by the stewardess, he turned and let his eyes rest carelessly on the gray man. For just an instant their glances crossed and McBride's stomach quivered slightly. He hoped the gray man would never have reason to dislike him. He hoped that if the gray man ever found a reason that he, McBride, would have a gun in each fist and that the gray man would be bound hand and foot.

It wasn't that the gray man looked ferocious. Rather, he had a genius for utter quiet. The grayish, not unhealthy pallor of his face was but another shade of the varying grays which clothed him. Even his shoes were gray. His hair, parted in the exact center and combed flatly back, was polished pewter, and the very small mustache was a thin gray line across the lighter gray of his upper lip. McBride thought the mouth had never smiled. He thought the eyes did, as they met his, bleakly, a little mockingly.

He went on to the lavatory. He was surprised to find that the palms of his hands were moist. He didn't know why this should be, because he had never seen the man before and probably should never see him again. He drank two glasses of water and told himself it must be the altitude. He went back to his seat.

The stewardess came and sat in her little nook next to the

lavatory door. She looked, McBride thought, a little like Sheila. Younger, not so poised, except in relation to her job, but she had the same coppery hair and the trick of letting her hands lie quietly in her lap.

He turned slightly, smiling at her. "Tired?"

"Not very."

"You through at Palos Verde?"

"No, I go on to Salt Lake."

"Too bad," he said. She colored faintly and this reminded him of Kay Ford. He said, "We'll make Verde on time?"

She looked at her strap watch, looked out and down at a flashing beacon. "In an hour."

He sighed and went to sleep. When he awoke she was bending over him, fastening the safety belt. For a moment he thought she was Sheila and he murmured, drowsily, "You're sweet."

"And you're a very fast worker," she whispered. Aloud she said, "Five minutes." The transport nosed down out of the clouds. McBride wondered if the gray man had been asleep too.

THE AIRPORT at Palos Verde was not like those around Los Angeles. There was no mosque-like administration building; there were no rows of shops, no concrete runways. Except for the great beacon and the border markers and the lone hangar, part of which served as the despatcher's office, there was nothing. They had removed the cactus and the Joshua trees; otherwise the desert was as God made it.

Two taxis and a hotel bus fought for the patronage of the five debarking passengers. The old lady with the Bible and the traveling salesman did not get out. The Queen of Diamonds chose a taxi. So did the blonde who was getting a divorce. That left the bus for the enormously fat man and the gray man and McBride. They got in. It was 12:45.

On the way into town none of the three said anything. In the darkness McBride felt that the other two were watching him. He lit a cigarette so that they could see it wasn't bothering him any. Palos Verde burst on the horizon like a hophead's dream of the Aurora Borealis. The town had mushroomed since McBride's last visit, which was to be expected. Fifteen or twenty thousand extra paychecks would boom Pittsburgh. Originally a division point on the railroad, with the major sports of gambling and quickie divorces as sidelines, Palos Verde had blossomed overnight into an industrial center. The greatest dam in the world was being built practically at its very gates. Palos Verde expanded its chest.

McBride and the fat man and the gray man got out under the marquee of the Hotel Grand National. McBride was the only one who went inside. He gave his bag and topcoat to the bell captain, stood partially concealed by a group of potted palms and watched the other two tip the driver of the bus. Each then went his separate way and was swallowed up in the maelstrom of lights and noise which was Grand Avenue.

McBride registered. "Room and bath, away from the street if possible."

The clerk looked at McBride's clothes. "We have a room at fifteen a day, Mr. McBride."

"Okay. What time does the limited get in from Los?"

"Four-fifteen."

"Call me at three-thirty."

"You're going out on that train?"

"No, just meeting it. I'll be here for some time." He tossed a fifty dollar bill on the counter, was pleased with the added deference the clerk evinced. He followed the bell-hop to the one elevator and was presently asleep in his fifteen dollar bed. He dreamed that he was rescuing the airplane stewardess from the unwelcome attentions of the gray man. When he awoke his forehead was beaded with sweat.

The phone was ringing. Without turning on the light he answered it. The clerk's voice said, "Three-thirty, Mr. McBride."

"Oh, thanks." He snapped on all the lights and went into the bath and showered. Dressing, he considered his reflection in the mirror and again thought that perhaps he was being a very great fool. On the other hand the Irish, especially the Black Irish, had been known to have hunches. McBride liked to play his hunches. He went down to the lobby and through that to the bar. Apparently no one but he had thought of sleeping. The town was wide awake and going strong. He had coffee and brandy, looked at his watch, decided he had time to walk to the station. He went out the side door into a dark cross street and presently emerged onto Grand Avenue.

The neon-lighted Palace Club was packed; so too was the Natividad and the Verde and all the others. Hard-bitten men in sweat-stained khaki and boots rubbed shoulders with white-faced men in tails and women who, had they been at home, wouldn't have touched them with a ten-foot pole. There is no leveler like the gambling table.

Taxis paraded the streets, and twelve-thousand-dollar limousines fought for places beside twelve-wheeled trucks labeled with the name of Leeds & Leeds. Except for the gaudy lights the city of Palos Verde was no different at four in the morning than at four in the afternoon. McBride walked quietly, unhurriedly through it all.

AT THE station he chose a vantage point away from the crowd which thronged the platform. He was consciously being very careful now. With the brick wall of the subjoined freight house at his back he took out his little gun and held it at his side. He didn't know what he expected to happen; he just thought that he would be ready in case anything did. The Limited rolled in.

There was quite a flurry for a while; people getting on and off; residents greeting newcomers; the rumble of baggage and mail trucks. McBride saw his own trunk unloaded. He brought his eyes back to the fifth Pullman behind the dining car because the vestibules of all the rest had been closed. A man hurried out of the car onto the platform and the porter reached for the man's bag. Two shots sounded, very close together. The man on the car platform staggered, sprawled headlong into the porter's arms. McBride ran around the freight house, toward the sound of the shots. The street looked exactly as it had before. There were plenty of people around, plenty of cars. There was no sign of the man or woman who had fired the shots; not even a wisp of smoke or the tang of cordite in the crisp sharp air.

Somewhere beyond the station a police whistle sounded. McBride dropped his gun in a side pocket, thrust his way back through the crowd. The porter and a conductor knelt beside the man who had fallen. Two bright crimson splotches showed on the breast of the man's topcoat. His eyes were wide open.

"He's dead," the conductor said.

McBride didn't say anything. He had just noticed that the dead man's build was very like his own; that hat, camel's-hair topcoat and even the pigskin bag could have passed for those of Rex McBride. He thought he was going to be very sick at his stomach. He went back to the hotel.

CHAPTER IV

ON THE GRILL

THE CHIEF OF police said, "Just what is your business in Palos Verde, Mr. McBride?"

"My own," McBride said. He was breakfasting in the hotel grill. It was eight-thirty in the morning. It had taken the cops four hours finally to get around to him.

The chief was a stocky man with thick arms and hair on the backs of his hands. A fringe of nondescript hair started above his left ear and went around an otherwise bald pate to his right ear. His eyes had the color and all the warmth of ball bearings. McBride's reply didn't please him.

He said, "Just a big-town boy, eh?" His right hand gestured faintly toward a big clown with a beer paunch under a gravy-spotted vest. Tubby had discovered McBride's overcoat on a costumer between two tables. He also discovered the .25 automatic in one of the pockets. He was quite a detective. He lumbered up with the coat and the gun.

The chief said, "Let's go down to Headquarters, McBride."

McBride wiped egg remnants off his lips with a napkin. "Sure." He drank the last of his coffee. Paying his check, he ogled the girl behind the cashier's wicket. "What else do you do beside cashier?"

"You'd be surprised, big boy." She was a blonde. McBride didn't like blondes very well. With the chief on one arm and Tubby on the other he went out to the street.

Palos Verde in the light of day was undeniably shabby. It had the littered look of an apartment after an all-night party. Jewelry stores made a great play on slightly used wedding rings. McBride thought that coming here for a divorce might be worse than living with the guy. Rumbling trucks raised dust eddies in the brick-paved street.

Police headquarters was a grimy artificial stone building less than a block from the railroad station. You had to go up half a dozen steps. In the corners of the steps debris had been allowed to accumulate for weeks. The desk sergeant inside needed a shave.

McBride and the chief and Tubby went into an office labeled *Chief*. McBride still didn't know the chief's name. He decided it must be a secret. The chief sat heavily in a swivel chair behind a scarred oak desk. Tubby leaned his back against the ground-glass panel of the door. He had a quill toothpick and he began plying this with great industry. McBride had never met a pair of cops who talked less.

The chief opened some mail, made disparaging noises with his lips, looked out the window, finally got around to looking at McBride. "There was a guy killed down at the station this morning."

"You don't say!"

"Yep."

Tubby sucked at a cavity he couldn't reach with the toothpick. After a while he said, "You were there."

McBride pretended great annoyance. "How did you find out?"

Both recited as if by rote: "You came in on the 12:40 plane, registered at the Grand National, left a call for 3:30. You told the clerk you were meeting the train."

"And did I meet it?" McBride asked mockingly.

"You did."

"All right," McBride said, "I did. I saw the guy get his, and I tried to locate the guy that gave it to him. I couldn't, so I went back to the hotel." He felt pleasantly virtuous. There is nothing like telling the truth to make you feel virtuous.

The chief nodded as if things were coming along very nicely indeed. His eyes met McBride's suddenly. "You left out a couple of things. The dead guy was wearing clothes a lot like yours. Maybe somebody thought he was you."

"Why should they?"

"That's what we're trying to find out," the chief said. He looked at the dust motes climbing in a bar of sunshine. From behind McBride Tubby said, "Why were you meeting that train?"

"I like to meet trains," McBride said.

The chief flexed his tonsils. "I don't like your attitude, McBride. We're trying to solve a murder."

"That ought to be a novelty," McBride said. "I hear there have been a lot of them around here lately."

TUBBY moved ponderously toward him. When their feet almost touched, Tubby took the toothpick out of his mouth, looked at it, put it back again. Then he hit McBride in the eye. McBride sat down on the floor.

The chief made clucking noises. "Now, now, Harry."

Tubby looked disappointed. "He's a pushover, that's what he is. I hardly hit him at all." He retreated to the door.

McBride dabbed a handkerchief at his eye. There was no blood. He got to his feet, slapping the dust from his bottom.

The chief said, "You're a dick, aren't you, McBride?"

"I used to be."

"License to work in this state?"

"No."

"Then don't work," the chief said. He looked at the little gun they had taken from McBride. "I'll keep this till you're ready to leave town. Maybe it wouldn't be such a bad idea at that."

"Is that an order?"

The chief looked at Tubby. "Do you think it should be an order, Harry?"

Tubby spat. "Let him stick around a while. He might be fun." He looked wonderingly at his right fist. "His eye ain't even gonna get black."

McBride stooped and picked up his hat and put it on. He got his camel's-hair off the desk, draped it carefully over an arm. At the door he turned. "The dead guy?"

"He was a hardware salesman."

"And your name?" McBride said.

"Beale," the chief said. "Jim Beale."

McBride's eyes smouldered as they rested on Tubby. "His name's Beale too," the chief said. "We're brothers."

"Thank you," McBride said. He went out.

AT THE hotel he found that his express receipt had come in with the morning mail. The clerk said, "There was a telephone call for you, Mr. McBride." He pulled a slip of paper out of McBride's pigeon-hole. There was nothing on it but a Palos Verde number. McBride went into a phone booth and called the number.

Almost instantly a man's voice answered. "Is this Mr. McBride?"

McBride said that it was. "Mr. Rex McBride?" the voice insisted. When McBride admitted that the man was right on both counts the man sighed audibly.

"This is no doubt very nice of you," McBride said. "Very few people are relieved to find I'm around. Mind telling me to whom I owe all this solicitude?"

"This is Leeds, McBride. Colin Leeds of Leeds & Leeds."

"I've heard the name," McBride said.

There was a sort of stunned silence at the other end. Then, irritably: "Do you realize that we've been worried sick about you? That—that man who got off the train. I thought it might be you."

"Why should you think that?"

"Because we heard you were coming in on that train, of course!"

"Oh, of course," McBride said. He thought, "No wonder the others were killed. You might as well be a goldfish." Aloud he said, "Assuming you are as interested in my health as you pretend to be, the little incident down at the station should suggest something to you."

"Such as what?"

"That you mind your own damned business!" McBride yelled. "I don't want any part of you!" He banged the receiver into its hook, banged the door open.

The girl at the switchboard looked at him. "Bad news?"

"That's all I ever get," McBride said. He went into the bar and sulked over a Collins. He was not conscious of the gray man's presence until the gray man actually stood at his elbow, ordering sherry and bitters in a voice as musical as Westminster chimes. McBride's stomach crawled.

The bartender said, "How's tricks, Mr. Train?"

"Tricks," the gray man said, "are very good indeed, Charlie." He turned his eyes obliquely on McBride's profile. "Staying in town long?"

McBride looked at the Collins in his right hand. He was surprised to see that it was quite steady. "It depends," he said, "on how lucky I am."

"You're a gambler, then?"

McBride nodded.

"I'm a gambler too," the gray man said. He took a silver dollar out of his pocket. "Care to match for the drinks?" He spun the dollar on the bar in invitation. "Heads," McBride said. It came tails. Mr. Train picked up his dollar, drained his glass and went out of the bar as quietly as he had come in. McBride pushed his half-finished drink across the bar. "Weak," he said.

The barman was indignant. "The Collins?"

"No, me." He thought he looked a little pale in the mirror. After a while he said, "Who is that guy?"

"Mr. Train?" Charlie swabbed a spot on the mahogany left by the gray man's sherry and bitters. "Why, everybody knows Mr. Train. He runs this town."

"Oh," McBride said. He wondered if the gray man had attended personally to the hardware salesman, or if he'd just hired it done. He had the feeling that more than the two guesses were not justified. He went up to his room. Someone had done a thorough job searching it.

CHAPTER V

FOURTEEN DEAD MEN

WITH HIS LUNCH McBride absorbed a few facts on the current scene. He had the Palos Verde *Argus,* the Palos Verde *Inquirer* and the *Mining & Engineering Journal.* He learned that the Palos Verde dam, when completed, would impound so many millions of acre-feet of water; that it was to be taller than the Empire State Building; would be six hundred feet thick at its base and have a five-lane highway on its crest. He learned that the developed power would supply three states; that the water rights had finally been more or less amicably allocated; that the total cost was just under a hundred and eighty million dollars. He thought that was a lot of money.

The hardware salesman's name was Cunius. It was thought that the police would have his murderer in custody within twenty-four hours. He had been a regular visitor to Palos Verde and it was believed that possibly he had made enemies.

Colin Leeds, of Leeds & Leeds, General Contractors, said that the work was progressing nicely; that accidents and delays were always to be expected at the outset on a project of this size, but that the situation was now well in hand.

A Mexican named Gonzales had been found in the washroom of the Palace Club with a knife in his back. Foul play was suspected, though it was hinted that he may have been despondent over losses sustained at the faro bank. The article didn't attempt to explain how he could have driven the knife into his own back.

There was a picture of the enormously fat man who had occupied the seat in the plane directly in front of McBride. Under the picture was the caption, *Genial Host at Club Natividad Predicts Bumper Tourist Crop.* The guy's name was Van. McBride didn't think he looked very genial.

Under Vital Statistics McBride read: *Divorces granted, 17; Marriage licenses issued, 17; Births, none; Deaths, 5.* At this rate even the desert air wasn't going to save Palos Verde from ultimate extinction. McBride wondered if the *Deaths, 5* included the hardware salesman, or if he was an extra. He felt rather badly about the hardware salesman. He thought that if he, McBride, had taken the train instead of the plane the hardware salesman might be still alive.

He signed his check and got up and went out and made a reservation for the two o'clock rubberneck bus to the dam site. The house detective engaged him in conversation. McBride had made quite a beef about having his room searched. "Funny thing," the house dick said, "we ain't had nothing like this happen for months."

"That's the McBride luck for you," McBride said. He brightened. "I guess I was lucky at that. My trunk hadn't got here yet."

The house man looked suspicious. "You mean there was something really valuable in your trunk?"

"Eight grand, is all."

"No!"

"Fact," McBride said. He was wearing gray tweeds now, and carried a light tweed topcoat. He took a Manila envelope from an inside pocket. "Think I'll put it in the safe."

The dick's eyes got very round. "What's the idea carrying so much cash?"

"In my racket," McBride said, "you need cash."

"That reminds me, Mr. McBride, just what is your—uh—business?"

"I'm a labor organizer," McBride said. He let his left eyelid droop slightly. "Keep it under your hat, will you?" He felt the guy's eyes follow him all the way over to the desk. He left the Manila envelope with the clerk.

The girl at the switchboard gave him the eye. She had a large green florist's box and was whistling a little tune against the edge of McBride's card. She said, "What do I do to earn this?"

"Think of a number," McBride said.

She thought.

"Now double it."

She closed her eyes, calculating. "The answer," McBride said, "is just one of the numbers I am not going to call. The ones I do call you are supposed to forget, or fake, in case anybody should ask you afterward. Catch?"

"I catch," she said.

HE WENT into a booth and closed the door. After a moment or two he was talking with Louie Orsatti in Los Angeles. "McBride, Louie. I won some dough in your place yesterday."

"You're telling me!"

"Did I do any talking; say anything about taking a trip?"

"No."

"In case anybody asks you, Louie, I'm just a guy who likes to roll 'em."

"You in a jam?"

"No."

"Okay," Louie sighed. "When do I get a crack at that four grand you took me for?"

"Hah-hah," McBride said. He hung up and called the austere chairman of the board of Acme Indemnity, Mr. Franz Charles, also in Los Angeles. He was not cordial to Mr. Charles. "Listen, you guys want to get me killed?"

"Certainly not," Charles said stiffly.

"Well, you've been doing your best. I thought this was supposed to be a confidential job."

"I don't understand you, McBride."

"Who told Leeds & Leeds I was coming up here?"

"I don't know. It may have been I, or Rourke, or one of the others. The senior Mr. Leeds dropped in just after you left. We thought that perhaps if you had some kind of a job on the project—"

McBride cursed. "What do I know about dams? Do I have to push a wheelbarrow to find out what's going on? Look, there was a guy killed here this morning. He was supposed to be me. You know why he was killed? Because someone in your gang, or in Leeds & Leeds, shot off his mouth."

"McBride, you don't suspect—"

"It happened, didn't it?"

"But it don't make sense, man! The Alliance and Leeds & Leeds are working together on this thing."

"Okay, it don't make sense." Neither does a dead shamus. So here's what I'm going to do. I'm going out and send you a wire, resigning. You let Leeds & Leeds and the whole world know that I've resigned. Maybe one will cancel the other."

Charles said, "The wire will be camouflage, McBride?"

"I don't know. Maybe I'll mean it."

"So you're afraid!"

"You're damned right I am," McBride said. He banged up the receiver. After a moment he called the same number again. This time he asked to be connected with Miss Kay Ford. "Kay, honey? Rex McBride. How are you?"

Her voice sounded golden warm. "Rex, how nice!"

"Busy tonight?"

"Why no, nothing that I couldn't postpone. You don't mean you're coming back so soon?"

"Yes, I'm washed up here. At least as far as the Alliance is concerned. I've run into something that means more money."

"Oh?"

"Yes," he said. "Maybe I'll tell you about it when I see you. Seven o'clock?"

"Seven o'clock," she agreed. When he came out of the booth

he didn't know whether he had been smart or not. One thing sure, though, by the time the various bits of news he'd spread began to get around, no one could be positive about anything. Not even that his right name was Rex McBride. He crossed the street to the telegraph office and sent an insulting resignation to the Alliance of Pacific-Southwest Underwriters. He neglected to mention their five thousand dollars, considering this unimportant.

AT FIVE minutes of two he climbed on the rubberneck bus. It was pretty well filled. Van, the very fat and allegedly genial host at the Club Natividad, apparently had known what he was talking about. The bus load was typically tourist. A sprinkling of serious-minded schoolteachers weighted the preponderance of callow youths and sweet young things from neighboring dude ranches. Mr. Average Citizen, as pictured in the cartoons, explained things he knew nothing about to his middle-aged and slightly palpitant wife. The air was sharp and crisp and crystal-clear.

The highway led straight across the desert floor, dwindling gradually in the perspective of twenty-five miles but distinct and sharply etched until it was swallowed up by the first low rise of foothills. Two or three miles distant and paralleling the highway a freight train crawled. The conductor-guide raised his megaphone. McBride shut his ears against the sound.

So far his investigation, if it could be called that, had netted him nothing beyond the profound conviction that his predecessors hadn't died or become discouraged through lack of attention. This led inevitably to the conclusion that there was monkey business afoot. In other words, there was a sinister purpose behind some if not all of the accidents. They'd built the Golden Gate Bridge with one tenth the loss of life; one tenth the damage to materials and equipment. Here, all they had to do was plug up a river. McBride, not being an engineer, considered a bridge, any bridge, of infinitely greater importance than a dam.

He brought his mind resolutely back to the problem as it concerned him personally. It was easy enough to see who stood to lose by all the delays and unwelcome publicity. Leeds & Leeds would suffer most, and back of them the Pacific-Southwest Underwriters. The Alliance had underwritten the entire project, but naturally not for full face value. Say sixty per cent. The government certainly wouldn't lose. They were protected by bond and a forfeiture clause. So Leeds & Leeds stockholders could, within the realm of possibility, take it on the chin to the tune of forty per cent of a hundred and eighty million dollars; roughly, seventy million. Seventy million dollars, McBride decided, was not potatoes. Then why would Leeds & Leeds, or the Alliance, jeopardize their interests by blabbing to all and sundry about McBride? There was no logical answer to this. Inside either organization there could, of course, be spies working for the other side.

"What other side?" McBride demanded irritably. He wasn't aware that he had spoken aloud until the guy with the megaphone glared at him. He pulled his hat down over his eyes and wriggled lower in his seat. The monologue up front continued. McBride was beginning to acquire a headache. His mind pushed at the blank wall in front of it. Now then, who stood to gain by the sabotage at the dam? In terms of money he couldn't think of anyone but the Five Companies, who had bid against Leeds & Leeds and lost. Except in case of absolute collapse of the project the Five Companies couldn't hope to get a finger in this particular pie. But by the judicious expenditure of money they could make this pie look so messy that Leeds & Leeds would never get another chance at a job this size. And there were bigger and better jobs ahead. The government, like beavers, was dam conscious.

Okay, you had the Five Companies. In addition, there was the stock angle. Given the right amount of foresight a smart guy with money could utilize the present stink to make a nice profit out of manipulating Leeds & Leeds stock. McBride let this idea ride, because there were too many smart guys with money for him to investigate. Then there was the personal hatred, or revenge motive. McBride rather liked this idea because it came closer to home. It was something that he, being McBride, could understand. But no matter how you figured it, this was one case where you couldn't start at the top. You picked up the loose ends first and worked toward the middle. He was returning to Los Angeles to see if Kay Ford wasn't one of the loose ends. He thought, a very little, about Sheila Mason.

THE BUS rolled into the reservation and everybody got out. It looked a little like Camp Kearny at the beginning of the war, only not so self-conscious. The big shots, the resident engineers, were housed in immaculate, tile-roofed buildings, complete with lawns, shrubs and flowers, as though ordered from a catalogue. The workmen's barracks were already beginning to need paint. Shops, material yards and the railhead were conspicuously neat. The guide led his flock into the administration building where there was a scale model of the dam. McBride strolled casually away.

A guy with a rifle stepped out of a guard tower. "Have you a pass?"

McBride said that he hadn't. He said, "I'm with the rubberneck outfit."

The guard inclined his head. He was a very polite guy. "Just stay with the group and you will see all that is to be seen."

McBride showed his teeth in a brief smile. "No stragglers, eh?"

"No stragglers," the guard agreed.

McBride lit a cigarette. It appeared that this too was *verboten*. He stepped on the cigarette. Mid-afternoon sun made a glory of the tall hills and the vast sweep of the desert, and against these all man-made things became dwarfed; the giant steel towers and the cables looping between them, cables thicker than McBride's body, and the great monorail cars suspended over nothingness. The dam became a puny thing, and the men who plotted it, pygmies. McBride thought that perhaps he was the littlest pygmy of them all.

Inside the guard tower a bell rang stridently. The man with the gun went in. When he came out his face was chalk-white and he trailed his rifle as though it were a broken stick.

McBride said, "Trouble?"

The man stared at him with unseeing eyes. "Diversion tunnel 3," he said. "Cave-in."

McBride wet his lips. "How many men?"

"Fourteen," the man said.

CHAPTER VI

THE TEMPTRESS

SHE WAS THE same stewardess. She said, "You must think this is a taxi." McBride was the only westbound passenger. The girl sat across from him and the late afternoon sun slanted down on her coppery hair and clear skin. Again the quiet of her hands reminded him of Sheila.

After a while he said, "The gray man—does he ride with you often?"

"Mr. Train? No, not often. He has interests in Los Angeles that take him there two or three times a month."

"What kind of interests?" He didn't realize how sharply he had spoken till he saw slow color rise in her cheeks. He said, "I'm sorry. I didn't mean to snap at you."

She let her breath out slowly. "You're rather an abrupt person, aren't you? I don't know what Mr. Train's business is. You merely hear things about more or less regular passengers; you know, loose bits of gossip that rarely mean anything. He scarcely ever speaks to me."

"And the very fat man?"

"I've seen him once or twice before," she admitted. "He is a gambler. I don't like him very well."

"That makes two of us," McBride said. "Just the same, if you ever have to make a choice about who to run from, you run from the gray man and run like hell."

She looked at him curiously. "What did he ever do to you?"

"He won a drink from me this morning," McBride said. He

didn't tell her that the gray man scared him silly; that his fear antedated the silver dollar episode by several hours; that it had sprung, full-blown, from nowhere the minute he'd laid eyes on the guy and that he had never felt this same fear before. That was the hell of being Irish. You felt things. You felt that here was a man as impregnable, as unassailable as Gibraltar. The gray man could put a curse on you without saying a word.

McBride took off his hat, scowled at it. His expression was that of a little boy being a very fierce Indian. Presently he caught her amused glance on him and grinned sheepishly. "What's so funny?"

"You are," she said. "Will you be riding back with us tonight?"

He nodded. "I think so."

She went to the pilot's compartment. She didn't reappear until the airport beacon was directly beneath them.

The big ship squatted down in the middle of a light ground fog. McBride, descending, shrugged into his topcoat and gave his bag to a redcap. The girl, passing him with the pilot and co-pilot, touched his arm lightly. "Good night, Mr. Smith."

He'd forgotten he'd ever used the name. He remembered suddenly that he hadn't used it coming back. He went into the rotunda flower shop and ordered violets. "For the hostess on Number Seven," he said. On one of his own cards, under the McBride, he wrote, *"nee Smith."* He then went into a phone booth and loosed an avalanche of abuse on the florid Mr. Erin Rourke, Vice President of Acme Indemnity.

"Gentlemen," McBride reminded him, "don't shoot off their mouths. You tell anybody else who I was or what I was trying to do? You tell that dame you were with?"

Rourke's voice became ponderous with dignity. "It happens that I didn't, but what difference does it make now? I understand you've quit."

"For once you've understood something," McBride said. "But a guy died this morning and I'm looking for the so-and-so that shot him."

"So help me, McBride, I know nothing about it!"

"You could have left off the last two words," McBride snarled. He hung up, banged out of the booth, reëntered it and dialed Sheila's number. The quiet composure of her voice, so close to him, started his hands to shaking. "Rex, Sheila."

"Yes, dear?"

He was curiously hesitant after that. "May I see you for a little while?"

"Of course. Dinner?"

"Why couldn't this have been last night?" he thought. He tried not to let the thought seep through into his voice. "Well, no, dinner is out, I guess. I've some business. But if I could stop by for a few minutes—"

"Of course, Rex." It was she who broke the connection this time. Typical, he thought. Any other gal would let me do the hanging up. Trouble is, I don't really want any gal but you.

OUTSIDE, he yanked his bag out of the redcap's hand, was immediately sorry, apologized and gave the guy a dollar instead of his customary two-bits. He gave the hacker Sheila's address and settled back in the cab knowing himself for a heel. It lacked twenty minutes of being seven o'clock. He was going to be late for his date with Kay Ford. Well then, let her wait, he thought. I won't go to see her at all. In the same breath he knew that he was lying. He would see her.

The cab halted before Sheila's apartment. McBride got out, leaving his bag with the driver. "I'll be fifteen minutes or so. Wait." He went inside. There was no desk. It was just a good address for moderately well-to-do professional people. He used one of the two automatic lifts to take him up to the third floor.

Standing outside Sheila's door he thought he heard a man's voice inside. He pressed the buzzer. After a moment Sheila opened the door.

"Hello, Rex."

Looking over her shoulder, past the small foyer, he saw that he had not been mistaken. There was a man in the living room. He was an elderly man, somewhere in his late sixties. He was in evening clothes and he wore his white mustaches with a sort of Prussian militarism.

McBride said, "Who is that?"

He would have told you there wasn't a jealous bone in his body, but his manner, the tone of his voice, gave the impression that he was an outraged husband. He found himself flushing under Sheila's calm gray eyes.

She said, "It's just Mr. Leeds, Rex."

"What's the matter, can't he take care of his business with you during business hours?"

Two spots of angry color burned high up in her cheeks. "I think perhaps you had better go now, Rex."

"No, I'm coming in."

Wordlessly she stood aside. He went past her into the living room, removing hat and topcoat as he went. Sheila, following him, had a puzzled frown on her face. McBride could see she thought he was drunk. He said, "I'm not," just as though she'd spoken the words aloud. He stood there, staring insolently at the elder Leeds.

Sheila, very angry now, murmured the introductions. "Mr. Leeds—Mr. McBride."

McBride stuck out his hand automatically. Leeds ignored it. "I'm not in the habit of shaking hands with cowards," he said.

"Then you're not in the habit of shaking hands with honest men," McBride said. "A guy who tells you he's never been afraid is a liar."

Sheila said sharply, "Rex!"

Leeds said, "Men have been known to go on even though they were afraid."

"But not with their own side spotting them," McBride said. "A guy who does that isn't a hero. He's just a plain fool." He turned hot eyes on Sheila. "Has Leeds told you there was a guy killed this morning? A guy that was mistaken for me?"

She paled slightly. "I—I heard, Rex. I'm sorry."

"All right, you're sorry. I'm sorry too, because the guy hadn't done a thing in the world to anybody. All he did was to happen to wear the same kind of clothes I do, and now he's dead. You know why he's dead? Because someone who knew I was going to Palos Verde told someone else. How do I know it wasn't Leeds?"

"Rex, you must be out of your mind!"

"Not any more, I'm not," he said. He faced the older man. "See here, I didn't come here to quarrel with you. In fact I had no idea you were here at all; but as long as we're both here I'm giving you a piece of free advice. Close down the job till you get things ironed out."

Leeds sat down quite suddenly, as though all the strength had gone out of his legs. His face was haggard. "I can't, McBride."

"Fourteen more guys got theirs this afternoon," McBride said.

"Do you think I don't know it? Do you think my son Colin doesn't know it? He's on the verge of collapse."

"But he doesn't seem to be in any *personal* danger," McBride said nastily. "For that matter, neither do you. It's pretty nice to sit up in your upholstered offices and send suckers like me out to do your dirty work. Well, you can do your own from now on. I told the Alliance I was through and I meant it."

Leeds raised haunted eyes. "You're right, of course." He ran his tongue over parched lips. "What I said a moment ago—about your being a coward—I'd like to retract that, McBride. I'm sorry."

McBride felt Sheila's eyes on him, urgent. "Okay," he said gruffly, "forget it. I'm sorry for some of the things I said too, or at least for the way I said them. But they were the truth." He looked at Sheila. "See you alone for a minute?"

He picked up his hat and coat, started for the door. Something, a hunch perhaps, caused him to halt abruptly and look back at the white-haired Leeds. "What do you know about a guy named Train?"

The question was like a shot in the arm. The old man stood up so suddenly that his chair crashed back against the wall. "The man is a devil!"

McBride nodded. "That was my impression too. Is he responsible for what's going on?"

Leeds bent to straighten the chair. It was as though he used the gesture to mask some inner struggle. When he again faced McBride all signs of his previous agitation had vanished. "I don't know, McBride. Offhand I'd say no."

"I understand he has interests here in Los Angeles."

"That is true. He is on the boards of several corporations; he's a director of the Third National Bank."

"Your bank?"

"One of them." Leeds put suddenly blazing eyes on McBride. "What's all this to you? I thought you were through."

"And you thought right," McBride said. "I was just checking up on my future employer."

Sheila uttered a little cry of dismay. Leeds stared at him dully for an instant; then, as McBride's meaning penetrated his shock, he said, quite distinctly, "I hope you rot for that." He turned his back and walked deliberately to the windows.

IN THE foyer Sheila clutched McBride's arms. "Rex, you can't mean that. You can't!"

He wanted to tell her that he didn't; that it was all just an act. He wanted to take her in his arms and tell her not to worry, that everything was going to be okay. And he knew that if he did this, even with Sheila, he would be right back where he'd started—behind the eight-ball. He said, meaning it but not realizing how it would sound to her, "Marry me, kitten, and we'll call the whole thing off."

She struck him across the face. He stared at her unbelievingly for an instant. Then without a word he went into the hall.

Downstairs, his cab was still waiting. Ten minutes later he was standing before Kay Ford's door.

Miss Ford opened to his ring. She was wearing a green velvet hostess gown and her blue-black hair was done high on her head. Her eyes were dark blue pools. She was the most beautiful thing he had ever seen. He took her face in his two hands and kissed her.

She pushed him away, laughing. "My, what a robust greeting!"

"I'm glad to see you," he said. He was, too.

The door across the hall opened and an old lady with curlers peered out at them. "Oh, excuse me!"

McBride lifted his hat politely. "Think nothing of it, ma'am."

She shut her door hastily. McBride followed Miss Ford into the living room. Again he was impressed with the luxury of this apartment as compared to Sheila's. He knew that Sheila as an attorney on the legal staff of Leeds & Leeds must be making more than any secretary he had ever heard of. Except, maybe, the president's. And Sheila wasn't one to skimp, either, yet she certainly didn't have anything like this, or like Kay's clothes.

McBride sank luxuriously into a white, uncut-mohair divan. She sat beside him. "Tell me about it."

He told her what he thought was good for her to know. Flavored slightly with bits of truth, it made a good yarn. "I should walk around being a target," he said resentfully. "Besides, I ran into a guy I used to know. He's got a club in Verde and he offered me a chance to buy in. It's a good racket."

"Gambling?"

He grinned. "Not when you're working for the house. It's a sure thing."

"Would you like to have dinner here, Rex? I ordered some things sent in."

"Too much trouble," he said. "How near are you ready to go out?"

"Five minutes?"

"Okay, toots."

McBride chose the Vendome, because the Vendome was less than three blocks away. The music was always good and they served an excellent dinner. As they were being shown to their table by the *maitre* McBride chanced to lift his eyes from Miss Ford's back. At a table in the far corner sat Sheila Mason. Across from her was the military Mr. Leeds. McBride thought that Sheila's lips framed the one word, "Business!" Then she had turned away and was listening to something Leeds was saying.

McBride remembered that he had offered business as an excuse and hot blood flooded his face. Miss Ford, watching him, said, "Is she the one?"

He pretended to be very dumb. "Is who the one what?"

Quite deliberately she opened her bag, took out cigarettes and a long amber holder. She fitted a cigarette into the holder. "The gal with the frighteningly gray eyes." She leaned across the table for his light. "Lovely hair, too. Only," she added, "I thought you preferred dark hair."

He scowled. "I do." He yawned widely. "I met her a couple of times on a case I was working. Her husband was a louse."

"Was?"

He nodded. "Unh-hunh. He died of tuberculosis and a couple of complications. The complications were .45 slugs. I shot the guy that gave it to him, though I still don't know why."

Miss Ford sampled her soup. "Isn't that the senior Mr. Leeds with her?"

"By me," McBride said. He drank his cocktail hurriedly, stood up. "I just remembered something. I've got to make a phone call." He draped his napkin over the back of his chair. "Mind?"

"Not at all." She wasn't even looking at him as he went out of the dining room and into the lobby. There were three phone booths, all empty. McBride ignored them, went into the men's room, through that to the bar and thence out to the street. He walked rapidly toward Kay Ford's apartment house.

Her door was on the latch. McBride had thoughtfully arranged that on leaving, by reaching behind him and depressing the button. He went in and clicked on all the lights and began a thorough, though somewhat hasty search, of the rooms. He didn't find anything. He was straightening a picture on the living room wall when the hall door opened.

Miss Ford stood there. She had McBride's coat and hat. She said, "I paid the check."

He grinned disarmingly. "You're a smart gal, Kay."

She moved slowly into the room. "I manage."

"And how," he said.

She put his coat and hat down on a chair. "Find what you were looking for?"

She dropped her own wrap carelessly on the white rug, sank back on the divan. "Come here," she said, and when he was beside her: "You needn't have done this to me, Rex. I'd have told you anything you wanted to know."

CHAPTER VII

MORNING AFTER

McBRIDE WAS MAKING coffee in his kitchen. He had showered and shaved and put on a clean shirt from his bag and altogether he was feeling pretty good, considering. It was eight o'clock in the morning. The sun was shining and the birds were singing lustily in the park opposite, and McBride, watching the coffee pot do its stuff, whistled through his teeth and reflected cheerfully that this, his latest trip to Los Angeles, had not been without its compensations. He now had any number of logical reasons for returning to Palos Verde. Starting with the hotel dick at the Grand National, the hotel there, he had become a labor organizer, a prospective employee of Mr. Train (the gray man), and a partner in a gambling club. He felt that one more reason would not be too many and he giggled a little, planning the modus operandi of becoming gunsel extraordinary to the Five Companies. This, he hoped, would enable him to get a permit to carry a gun. He was still mindful of Chief of Police Jim Beale and his fat brother Harry. He was, he vowed, going to catch Harry up an alley some dark night. After a while he called a cab and stopped by Kay Ford's apartment on his way downtown. It took her a long time to answer the doorbell. When he finally did she was still practically asleep. He said, "Time to get up, babe."

She opened one eye. "Go away."

"Unh-unh. Secretaries are always at their desks by nine. It's an axiom or something. You see 'em in the movies."

44

She opened both eyes. "What time is it?"

"Eight-thirty, hon, and papa's going bye-bye." He set his bag down, looking at her. She was wearing a pale green satin negligee trimmed with ermine. There were dark circles under her eyes. "Where are you going?"

"Palos Verde." He grinned at her.

"When are you coming back?"

He looked past her into the apartment. "When you get ready to tell me how you can do all this on a secretary's salary."

"I told you."

"About the rich uncle who died?"

She shrugged her beautiful shoulders. "All right, he wasn't an uncle."

"That's what I thought," McBride said. He pushed the door open a little wider with his foot. "Well, goom-bye, hon."

She lifted her mouth and he kissed her briefly. "You will come back, Rex? Promise?"

"Cross my heart," he said. Stooping to pick up his bag, he looked at her from under his tugged-down hat-brim. "It wouldn't be that old goat Franz Charles who pays for this dump?"

"No," she said, "it wouldn't. When you come back I'll show you my bank book."

"When I'm with you, hon, I don't seem to care about looking at bank books." He went out, down to the street, walked briskly over to Wilshire Boulevard and caught a double-decker bus. He rode the top deck, staring interestedly in all the second story windows. He was pretending very hard that he didn't care what Sheila Mason thought of him.

Downtown, he got off at Fifth and Hill and walked over to Spring and the heart of the financial district. None of the banks or the brokerage houses were open yet. He ate breakfast in Lacy's. Over his coffee he read that Leeds & Leeds Construction was off nine points. This, in view of yesterday's general market trend, looked very bad indeed. McBride ordered cigars with his second cup of coffee.

Louis Orsatti breezed in the front door, spotted McBride instantly and came over to his table. "Well, as I live and breathe!" Orsatti was fat and very affable, even to his enemies. He wore a beautifully tailored morning coat, striped trousers and spats.

"Sit down," McBride said. "Have a cigar."

Orsatti sat down. He said, "Now look, if this is a touch the answer is no. Why do you suppose I'm down here so early? I'm trying to make an honest dollar in the other guy's racket."

"The market?"

Orsatti nodded gloomily. "Couple guys welshed on their bets last night. All they could pay off in was tips."

"Sucker." McBride puffed great clouds of smoke. "You ought to try Palos Verde. From all I hear there's room for an honest game."

Orsatti shook his round head violently. "Not me. I like living. That town's sewed up tighter than seven hundred dollars."

"Train?"

"Unh-hunh."

"Scared of him?"

"You're damned right I am."

"Me too," McBride said. He puffed more smoke clouds. After a while he said, "Who's a good broker down here? A guy who can keep his mouth shut?"

"See Art Lawson. Tell him I sent you." Orsatti spotted one of the men he'd been waiting for, got up. "Well, keep your neck in one piece, McBride."

"Sure." McBride waited till the café had partially cleared before he got up and paid his check.

HE LOOKED up Art Lawson in the Financial Directory at the desk. Then he went up to the seventh floor of the Securities Exchange Building and saw Art Lawson himself. Lawson was glad, he said, to be of service to any friend of Louie Orsatti's.

*McBride yelled, put a hand on
the rail and vaulted down.*

He was a small man in his early thirties, very brisk. His office had the opulent air of a first rate stock juggler. McBride thought he was probably a crook, but as long as he wasn't investing any money he didn't care.

He said, "Guy named Train. Home town Palos Verde, Nevada. Heavy interests here in Los. I want to know if he's interested in selling Leeds & Leeds Construction short. If you get the dope, wire me at the Grand National in Palos Verde. Just say yes or no, only if it's yes you'd better give me dates and amounts and things. Don't mention Train or Leeds & Leeds. Whatever's right, I'll pay it."

Art Lawson said he would see what he could do. He said he was certainly glad to meet a man of Mr. McBride's caliber, and if Mr. McBride ever wanted to take a little flier in the market—

"Thanks, no," McBride said. "I'm a crap-shooter, myself." He descended to Spring Street and caught a cab and was driven down to the station where he boarded one of the new stream-liners. He judged that his friend, the transport stewardess, was probably in Salt Lake, Utah, about now, and anyway he was in no particular hurry. He slept all the way to Palos Verde, sort of storing it up against future needs. He expected a rather busy night ahead.

It was notable that though it was only three-thirty in the afternoon and broad daylight when he reached Palos Verde McBride descended on the wrong side of the train. He felt that he had muddied the situation enough to warrant his safety, at least for a while, but there was no use deliberately kicking Fate in the teeth. Rounding the tail end of the train he ran smack into Harry Beale. The fat cop still had his quill toothpick, and he was wearing a smugly satisfied look.

"Hi, there, McBride."

"Hello," McBride said. He tried to pass the fat man.

Beale blocked his path. He said, "We got the killer of that hardware salesman."

If he had intended to startle McBride he certainly was a success. McBride dropped his bag. "The heck you did!"

"Yep." Beale removed the toothpick, looked at it search-ingly. "Guy ran a retail hardware store here at one time. The salesman's firm closed him up. He always blamed the salesman for it."

McBride had a suddenly empty feeling in the pit of his stomach. Here he'd been building a case on the hypothesis that it was he, not the hardware salesman, who was the intended victim and now the job turned out to be strictly business. He was stubborn, though. "He confess?"

Beale lifted a ham-like fist, looked at it complacently. The fist had a couple of skinned knuckles. "Sure he confessed. Wouldn't you?"

"What's this guy's name?"

"Engstrom."

"He get a lawyer yet?"

"Sure, we let him have a lawyer after he sang." Beale chuckled. "He's gonna need a lawyer."

McBride breathed deeply through his nose. "And the name of this mouthpiece?"

"Flack. Ernie Flack." Beale's colorless eyes settled full on McBride's face. "You wouldn't be gettin' ideas, would you?" He laid a heavy hand on McBride's shoulder. "Because if you was, my advice is don't."

McBride shook him off. "Listen, you fat slob, when I want your advice I'll ask for it. And if you ever lay a hand on me again I'll push that toothpick out the back of your neck." He picked up his bag. He was breathing gustily, angrily. "You think I won't?"

Beale smiled placidly. "You didn't do so well yesterday."

"And you won't always be in your brother's office, either," McBride told him. "Think it over." He walked uptown and left his bag with the bell captain at the Grand National. Then he went out and located Ernie Flack, the guy Engstrom's attorney.

Flack was a weasel-faced man with a perpetually harried look, as though he was forever but one jump ahead of his creditors. He looked at McBride hopefully. McBride said, "You think Engstrom really did it?"

Flack lost his hopeful expression. "They got a confession, didn't they?"

"Sure," McBride said. "With a couple of bulls beating up on you a guy would confess to anything. I'd say I murdered my wife, even if I didn't have a wife. You talk to Engstrom himself?"

Flack avoided his eyes. "He wasn't able to talk when I saw him. He was drunk."

"Yeah, probably with blood." McBride didn't like this guy. On the other hand he'd been admitted as Engstrom's attorney and McBride wanted to see Engstrom. He took a hundred dollar bill out of his vest pocket. Flack's eyes glistened. "Look,"

McBride said carefully, "I've got a theory about this kill. Eng-strom's arrest blows it up. Let's go see Engstrom, hunh?"

Flack got up with a great show of interest. "You bet!"

"We'd better have a reporter too," McBride said. "Is there such a thing as an honest one in town?"

Flack said he thought he could locate an honest one. He used the telephone.

THE REPORTER was waiting for them on the littered stone steps. Flack introduced McBride and the three of them went inside. Chief Beale was not in sight. Neither was brother Pudgy-puss. Flack spoke to the somnolent desk sergeant. "I'd like to see my client, Sarge."

The sergeant champed on his unlighted cigar, eyeing McBride and the reporter. Finally he said, "Well, why not?" He waved in the direction of a stone corridor.

They went along this to a steel-barred door and a turnkey in greasy denim let them through. His feet made slapping sounds on the concrete floor. He was only mildly interested in the whole thing. McBride had the impression that the police de-partment didn't really come to life until after nightfall.

They halted before a cell exactly like the forty or fifty other cells. There was a guy on one of the bunks. He was a little guy and his face had been beaten until it was almost shapeless.

McBride slipped the turnkey a folded bill. "Open the door, punk. I want a look at this guy."

"Sure, pal, sure." Keys rattled. The turnkey retreated toward the far end of the corridor. He unfolded the bill, looked at it furtively. He seemed satisfied.

Attorney Flack cleared his throat. "Engstrom, here are some men want to talk to you."

The figure on the bunk stirred. "Again?"

McBride went in. "Just take it easy, pal. We're friends." McBride got him under the arms, stood him up and turned him toward the light of the one small window. He said, "Unh-hunh, I thought so. You were down at the station yesterday when it happened."

Engstrom shivered. "I told them that."

"But you didn't kill the guy," McBride said.

The bleary eyes looked at him with a new interest. Flack said excitedly, "McBride, do you realize what you're saying?"

McBride turned sultry eyes on him. "Do I look like the kind of guy who talks out of turn? I was down at the station myself. I know this guy didn't kill anybody because I was close to him. The shot came from the street."

The reporter came alive. "Well, blow me down!" He grabbed McBride's arm. "You'll swear to this?"

"And if necessary I'll find other people that saw him too," McBride growled. "All you've got to do is look. The cops weren't interested in looking."

Flack said, "We'd better see Chief Beale." He was nervous.

McBride carefully laid Engstrom back on the bunk. He said, "You guys can see Beale. You better see a magistrate too. If there's any argument you know where to find me." He walked out, went past the turnkey who looked at him out of the corners of his eyes, paused in front of the sergeant's desk. Here he opened a new pack of cigarettes, crumpled the cellophane wrap and ostentatiously threw it on the floor. The sergeant said, "You act like you was at home."

"I've been in worse jails than this." McBride said. "They weren't run by white men, though." He went out into the fading sunlight.

ACROSS the street was a three-story office building. Half of the ground floor windows bore gold-leaf lettering reading: *Field Offices, The Five Companies*. In smaller script: *Research, Engineering, Survey*.

McBride crossed the street. In the main office, behind a long railing, there were a lot of guys sitting at draughting boards. They didn't look very busy. He stopped before a horseshoe counter labeled *Information.* A middle-aged woman with a face like an axe said, "This is a survey office. All our purchasing is done through—"

"Thanks," McBride said. "If I ever decide to become a salesman I'll let you know." He laid one of his cards on the counter. "I want to see Carmichael."

"Mister Carmichael?"

"He's just plain Carmichael to me," McBride said. He smiled suddenly. "You can call him Mister if you want to."

She backed away from him as though she thought he was slightly mad. When she was at least six feet from the protective counter she turned and literally ran to a frosted glass door. All the draughtsmen became suddenly very busy indeed.

The door opened and the woman reappeared, like a cuckoo bird. Behind her a tall saturnine-faced man took shape. He looked at the draughtsmen first, then he looked out at the street. Finally he got around to looking at McBride. He crooked a finger.

McBride went through the swing gate in the rail. The woman gave him a wide berth, as though he might have germs. McBride put a little extra swagger into his walk, crossing the office. He shoved a hand at the saturnine man. "I'm McBride."

The man took the hand, shook it once, let it drop. "So what?"

McBride jerked his head at the inside office. "Shall we talk a little bit?"

"About what?"

"About you and me and sudden death, maybe." McBride had his right hand in a topcoat pocket. There was nothing in the pocket but the hand. Carmichael backed into the office. McBride closed the door. Carmichael sat down at his desk. McBride stood by the windows. His teeth made a sudden flash of white in the semi-gloom. "I had an idea you'd be afraid, Carmichael."

Carmichael's face was lean and brown; his hands on the desk before him were lean and brown. Black eyes were set a little too close together but they didn't look the least bit afraid. He said, "What is your business with me, Mr. McBride?"

"What is your business in Palos Verde?" McBride countered. "Your outfit lost the bid on the dam job."

Carmichael nodded. "Quite true. There are things to be learned, though, by watching the other fellow's operations. We've been in the construction business a long time. We're still learning."

McBride said, "I've been in my business a long time, too."

"That reminds me, Mr. McBride. You haven't as yet stated your business."

"I'm a gunsel," McBride said. "A handy guy with a rod."

Carmichael yawned. "I don't believe I'd be interested."

McBride became very earnest. "I've been around town a couple of days. There's talk that maybe you are responsible for some of what's going on. Like that diversion tunnel cave-in yesterday. Fourteen guys just like that." He snapped his fingers. "Some of these workers don't think very well. They just get an idea and act on it without thinking. I thought maybe you could use a first class bodyguard."

Carmichael shook his head. "Still not interested."

"Okay," McBride sighed. "It's your neck, not mine." He swaggered out.

CHAPTER VIII

FAST ONE

THERE WAS A man sitting on McBride's bed. He didn't look dangerous. He looked, in fact, like a man who had just discovered the facts of life and was pretty bitter about it. He was just sitting there, not doing anything. The marks of his fingers were still plain on his forehead, as though he'd had his face buried in his hands for a while. He was a young-old man, somewhere in his late thirties, McBride judged. His very light hair was thinning on top. His skin was a rich mahogany brown, as though he'd spent a lot of time in the sun.

"Hello," McBride said.

"Hello," said the man. He didn't get up. "I'm Colin Leeds."

McBride closed the door carefully. He locked it. He then took off his coat and hat and hung them in the closet. His bag, he noted, had been brought up and placed on the luggage rack at the foot of his bed. There was no evidence that his room had been searched a second time. He sat in a chair across from Colin Leeds and lit a cigarette. He was mad, but he didn't show this. He looked like Sitting Bull, only younger. "How did you get in?"

"I bribed a boy for his pass-key."

"I see," McBride said. "The boy knew which room you were going to use it on?"

"No. No one at all knows that I am here. I remembered what you said when I telephoned you yesterday."

McBride let smoke out of his lungs. "Well, that's something."

Leeds stood up, began pacing the floor in short nervous strides. "I want to talk to you, McBride." When McBride didn't say anything to this he rushed on. He seemed in a great hurry to get it off his chest. "I know it was a great blunder for so many people to know about your coming up here. I'm sorry. But—I've been in communication with my father. You can't mean the things you said to him. You can't leave us flat this way."

"Can't I?" McBride said.

Leeds yanked at his tie, loosening it. "Look. I'm trying to tell you that this business is getting me down. I'm going nuts. I can't sleep, I can't eat." He dropped down on the bed again. "Do you know what it means to have a responsibility like mine? Did you ever have a lot of guys working for you and see 'em look at you as though you were directly to blame for killing their fellows? I'm an engineer. I'm supposed to be a construction chief. I'm not God."

McBride's eyes softened. He wished he could say something to this man that would ease his torment and still allow freedom of movement. He decided he couldn't. "What happened in that diversion tunnel yesterday?"

Leeds shivered. "We're blasting our way through solid rock. Four shots a day. It's possible that water seepage had something to do with it, that it just needed a heavy charge to shake the roof down. The thing that actually happened was that the shot went off too soon. The men weren't in the clear."

"What did the powder man say?"

"We had him up for questioning. He swore that he had been sitting right on top of his batteries; that he hadn't shoved the plunger home. Guys that reached him first said the circuit was still open. We couldn't prove otherwise. We fired him."

"That was smart," McBride said sarcastically. "What was this powder monkey's name?"

"Swiggart." Leeds' face was white, strained: "Look, McBride, I don't expect a lot from you. All I ask is that you give us what help you can. If it's money you want, just name it. Is it a deal?"

"No."

Leeds got to his feet. His eyes were crazy. "I guess my father was right. You're not only a coward, you're a lousy heel."

"All right," McBride said, "I'm a heel." He unlocked the door, looked up and down the corridor. There was no one in sight. "Now get out of here, and don't come back." He held the door wide.

LEEDS went out slowly, heavily, like an old man. McBride leaned his back against the closed door. He thought that probably he was going to be very sick at his stomach. He went over and lay face down on the bed for a while, until the nausea partially went away. It was black dark in the room when he finally got up and asked the desk to send him up a bottle and some ice. His stomach was still jittery. Anger, especially repressed anger, invariably did that to him. He wished he were a little angel, because angels were reported to never get sore about anything.

He turned on the lights, pulled his shades, stripped and went into the bath and climbed under the shower. When someone knocked loudly on the hall door he thought it was the bell-hop. He yelled, "Come on in," and wrapped a Turkish towel around his middle and went out to sign for the liquor. His caller wasn't the bell-hop. It was Chief of Police Beale.

McBride raised his right hand, palm out. His left clutched the towel about his naked loins. "How, Big Chief!"

Beale didn't think this was very funny. He said, "So you couldn't keep clean, hunh?"

McBride's face registered astonishment. "Me? What have I done now?" At Beale's curse McBride registered sudden understanding. "Oh, you mean about that little Engstrom guy? Why look, Chief, don't tell me you'd want to convict an innocent man. You wouldn't railroad a guy, would you?"

Beale's face turned a slow magenta. "You know so damned much, who did kill the guy, then?"

"I don't know, Chief, so help me I don't." McBride shrugged.

"Anyway, that's your worry, isn't it? The dead guy means nothing to me. I just happened to hear about Engstrom's being arrested—in fact it was your own brother told me—and so I dropped in to see the kind of heel that would do a thing like that. Imagine my surprise when—"

"Cut it, cut it!" Beale snarled. "You think I don't know what you did? You just dropped in, hunh? Like hell you did! You got the guy's mouthpiece and a newshawk before you made a move to go near Headquarters. You put me in a spot, that's what you did. I had to go out and find half a dozen other witnesses to prove my prisoner was innocent. And I had a confession!"

"By gosh, that's tough!" McBride said.

Beale took off his hat, crumpled it in his hairy paws. "You don't know just how tough, McBride. Not yet, you don't. You will, though, before I'm through with you. You think you can come into this town and set it on its ear, you got another guess coming."

"Now look," McBride said soothingly, "your idea about me is all wrong, Chief. I'm just a guy trying to get along, see?"

"Why did you quit the Alliance?"

"Oh, so you read a copy of my wire, did you?"

Beale flushed brick red. "Well, uh—"

"Never mind, Chief. I'd have done the same thing if I was a copper, wouldn't I? That's your job, to check up on strangers in town."

Beale grimaced as though he had a nasty taste in his mouth. "You heel, you haven't answered my question!"

"Oh, about why I quit? There's nothing to that. I just decided to quit, is all." He grinned. "Maybe you were partially responsible, at that. You sort of put ideas in my head, Chief. You know, about the hardware salesman being mistaken for me. I got to thinking the Alliance wasn't paying me to take risks like that."

There was another knock on the door. The bell-hop came in with a tray. McBride, clinging to the towel, signed the slip. "You'll find some change on the dresser, kid."

The boy set the tray down, helped himself to what he thought was about right, bobbed his head, went out. McBride said, "Have a shot, Chief?"

Beale looked at the label, ran a tongue over parched lips, looked at McBride, finally said, "Well, why not?"

"And a very good answer," McBride said. "Why not, indeed? You mix 'em, Chief. I'll be right out." He went into the bathroom. Coming out a couple of minutes later, in robe and slippers and with his wet hair neatly parted, he saw that Beale was not exactly a prohibitionist. The chief had a water tumbler full of straight rye. A lone ice cube fought valiantly to cool the liquor before it was all gone, but it was a losing battle. Beale emptied the tumbler without taking a breath.

"Bealsie," McBride said, "I salute you. You've got what it takes." He helped himself to a modest drink, proffered the bottle. "Go right ahead, Chief. It's a pleasure to watch you." Beale re-filled the tumbler. He drank. He said, "I'm drinking your liquor, but don't get the idea I like you. I hate you, see? And if you want to stay healthy, you keep your nose clean." His esses were slightly slurred, giving a shushing effect.

"That's all right," McBride said largely. "It takes a while to get used to me. You'll like me fine after we really get to know each other." He re-filled the chief's empty glass. Beale sat down suddenly in an upholstered chair. His ball-bearing eyes were glazed, like the patina on very old china. "No dinner," he mumbled. "Ain't had no dinner."

"Neither have I," McBride said. His mind was moving unhurriedly in an effort to fit this new development into a previously conceived plan. He said, "Tell you what we'll do. We'll finish up this bottle and then we'll have dinner together. Okay?"

Beale nodded gloomily. "Awright." McBride helped him find his glass, had another small shot himself, stood there looking down at the chief's bald spot. After a while he picked Beale up and laid him on the bed. The chief's breathing was faintly reminiscent of an underpowered switch engine pulling a heavily loaded drag.

McBride went into the bathroom, lifted the porcelain top from the flush box, bared an arm and reached down and got the spare gun he'd packed in his trunk. He dried it very carefully, examined the shells, decided he'd better replace them with new ones and got some out of the medicine cabinet. He then dressed, casting an occasional glance at the man on the bed. He estimated that he would have from a half to three quarters of an hour. He looked in the telephone directory for Mr. Carmichael's address. Then, using the back stairs and a villainous looking cab, he went out to the house.

IT WAS a fair-sized bungalow. It sat well back from the street, reserved, modestly sedate. Shrubs dotted the lawn, offering a certain amount of concealment. Three of the windows showed lights. The hacker didn't know that McBride was interested in the house. McBride had given him a random address in the next block. This turned out to be an apartment building.

McBride got out, said, "Wait, I'll be right back," and went into the building. He went right on down a long, carpeted hall to the service entrance. Debouching into an alley, dark as the inside of a black cat, he made his way swiftly and almost silently to the rear of Mr. Carmichael's bungalow. Crossing the back yard a malignant clothes line snatched his hat from his head and he lost a moment or two looking for it. Cursing, he took up where he had left off. One of the lighted windows belonged to a lady he took to be Mrs. Carmichael. Mrs. Carmichael was dressing for dinner. He went on to the next window, and here, though the blinds were drawn, he was rewarded with a beautiful silhouette of the saturnine Mr. Carmichael. McBride fired two shots through the glass. He then ran like hell. He was puffing so hard when he came out of the apartment house that he thought the cab driver would hear him.

The guy was looking down the tree-lined street. "You hear anything?"

"Yeah," McBride gasped. "Sounded like shots, didn't it?"

"I'll say it did!"

"Well, I don't want to get mixed up in it. Drive back to the hotel, only go around the other way." They drove back to the Grand National. It lacked a few minutes of eight o'clock when McBride let himself into his room. Chief Beale was still tearing it off. McBride went to the phone, ordered dinner for two. He then went into the bathroom and dropped the gun in the flush tank. As an afterthought he took a bar of soap and swished it around in the water till it looked like milk. He went out and looked with distaste at the inert figure on his bed, sighed, finally got a small phial of spirits of ammonia out of his bag and made a few tentative passes at the chief's nose.

Beale opened disillusioned eyes. "Oh, it's you!" He sat up. "What you trying to do to me?"

"Giving you an appetite for dinner," McBride said. He stared admiringly at Beale's flushed face.

"I get along," Beale said modestly. He wobbled into the bathroom and McBride could hear water splashing. After a while the waiters came up with the dinners. Chief Beale stuck his head out of the bath. His eyes glistened. The aroma of steak overpowered him. "I still hate you," he told McBride, "but you certainly do a guy well." They sat down to their steaks.

Approximately fifteen minutes later there was a knock on the door. It was the kind of knock you learn to associate with coppers. McBride was not too surprised when it was followed by the immediate and irate entrance of Harry Beale.

"Come in," he said, unnecessarily, because Pudgy was already in. "Come right in, Lieutenant!"

The fat man paused at sight of his brother. "What the hell, you been here all the time?"

The chief had a mouthful of steak. He swallowed this with great difficulty. "Now, Harry, now, Harry, don't go off half-cocked. Sure I've been here. Didn't I tell you I was coming up?"

Harry looked at McBride. "There's something screwy about this. You been here all the time too?"

McBride waved at the chief. "Ask him."

Chief Beale said McBride had never been out of his sight. He said irritably, "Come on, spill it, Harry. Don't stand there looking like a dissatisfied congressman. What's happened?"

The brother let out a string of obscenity. "Somebody took a couple of shots at Carmichael. Nearly got him, too."

The chief paled. "No! Why should anybody—"

"Shut up," his brother said. He looked at McBride. "Something smells around here and I think it's you, but—well, Carmichael wants you to call him."

"He tell you this personally? He tell you what it was about?"

Harry made unpleasant sounds with his fat lips. "Why else do you think I'm here, you dope? If my own brother didn't tell me it couldn't have happened I'd swear you framed this! I still think Carmichael is screwy to hire you, but it's his money."

"I'll need my gun back," McBride said. "And a permit."

The chief choked on a piece of steak. "In a pig's eye!"

Pudgy looked at him. "Carmichael says—"

Chief Beale got up hurriedly, wiping his lips. He shot an oblique glance at McBride's more or less innocent profile. "Well—" He looked around for his hat, found it, put it on. He went to the door. "Tell you what you do, McBride. Drop around at Headquarters after a while. We'll see what we can do."

He went out.

Pudgy smiled sleepily at McBride. "Keep on, just keep on." Then he too went out.

CHAPTER IX

POWDER MAN

IT TOOK McBRIDE quite a while to get a line on Swiggart, the powder man who presumably was not responsible for the explosion in Diversion Tunnel 3, yet who had been fired. He had to go about the thing cautiously. To admit he was a friend of Swiggart was to admit he had a grievance against Leeds & Leeds. To confess he suspected the man of complicity, or worse, was not liable to evoke any information in case the guy happened to have friends. Finally he got the address of a place on B Street that Swiggart was said to have visited occasionally. He went out there.

It turned out to be a honky-tonk, a sort of cross between a Yukon dance hall and the cheaper, if more modern, dive where the B girls roll you for all you've got and then have you thrown out for insulting them. There were a lot of colored lights, and a fair-sized dance floor, but the orchestra platform was empty. McBride guessed it was a quiet night. At the bar, three or four guys bought drinks for six or seven girls. There were more girls sitting in the booths at the far side of the big room. A drunk was dropping nickels in a player piano. Carpeted stairs led up to a second floor and McBride was just about to order himself a drink when a woman appeared at the head of the stairs. She was the striking white-haired woman whom he had seen on the plane the night before last; the one who wore all the mink and diamonds. Apparently his second guess about her had been the correct one; she certainly was not a dowager queen. She descended the stairs slowly. "Hello," McBride said.

She looked at him. "You've never been here before, have you?"

"My loss," McBride said. "I saw you on the plane the other night. I've been looking for you ever since."

She was the most self-possessed woman he had ever met. Her beautiful green eyes appraised him quite calmly, put an exact value on everything he wore, even down to his fifteen-dollar brogues. She said, "Don't kid me, Irish. I'm old enough to be your mother."

"But much too beautiful," he said. He nodded toward the bar. "I'll buy a drink, Queen."

She smiled then. "So you know my name too."

"Of course," he said. "You're the Queen of Diamonds." He took her arm. It was firm and round under his hand. He thought that the white hair was either synthetic or the result of something besides age. She raised her voice. "Folks, meet Irish. Irish, the folks. Irish is buying a drink."

Everybody crowded around. Everybody, including the drunk who was feeding nickels into the player piano, ordered. They toasted McBride noisily. The drunk went back to his nickel-dropping act and mechanical music blared in a continuous deluge from the speaker. The Queen of Diamonds went over and spoke to the drunk.

McBride paid for the first round, ordered another and picked himself a chair at an unoccupied table. A blonde girl came over and sat on his chair arm. "Stranger in town, honey?"

McBride admitted he was a stranger in town. He said, for her ear alone, "My pal Swiggart been around tonight?"

Her mouth drew down in a pout. "So you're here on business!"

"Monkey business," he agreed. "I owe the guy some dough. I want to pay him before you gals get it all." He fumbled his roll from a pants pocket and unostentatiously extended a creased twenty. Her hand covered it instantly. Her eyes watched the Queen of Diamonds with a scared look in them and when she spoke her lip scarcely moved. "The guy at the piano is Swiggart. Don't let on I told you."

*He caught a
flash of steel,
and struck with
his umbrella.*

McBride laughed loudly. "You're a card, babe, you certainly are a card!" He watched Swiggart drop another nickel in the slot. Music banged around the walls. A couple of the girls started dancing together. A bartender served McBride's drink at the table. The Queen of Diamonds said something in a low voice to Swiggart, came over and stood at McBride's side. "Having a good time, friend?"

"Swell," McBride said. He patted the table in time to the

music. His eyes admired the queen. "I could certainly go for you, though, Queenie."

Her green eyes warmed a trifle. "Some other time, Irish." She went into a room under the stairs. Everybody loosened up after that and it became quite a party. McBride crossed the room to the piano. Swiggart turned bloodshot eyes on him. He was a big guy, red-necked, heavy-faced. He wore good clothes sloppily.

McBride said, "Let's get out of here, mug."

"Why?" The guy wasn't as drunk as he looked.

"I'm working for Carmichael," McBride said. "The big shot with the Five Companies. Maybe I could do you some good."

Swiggart wiped his mouth on the back of a hand. "Carmichael, hunh? What kind of good?"

McBride looked around the room. "If there was some place we could talk—"

Swiggart said, "Okay, I know a place." He got his hat and coat off a chair. The door to the room under the stairs was open and McBride, passing it, saw that the room was an office. The white-haired woman was at the desk, using the phone. Her green eyes met McBride's and she flung the phone down and came toward him. "What's the matter, couldn't you find what you wanted?"

He grinned at her. "This guy and I just discovered we know each other. We're looking up a mutual friend."

"Coming back later?"

"Sure, Queen."

"Okay." She went back to her telephoning. McBride and Swiggart went out.

THIS dive was a remodeled house, the entrance above the street level, with stairs leading down to the sidewalk. Swiggart was a little ahead, halfway down the steps, when the shadow rose out of the area. McBride caught the dull sheen of metal in the shadow's hand. He yelled at Swiggart, put one hand on the iron rail and vaulted it. He plopped down on the man below, flattening him, just as the gun flamed. His big body helped muffle the sound. It was hardly more than a sharp handclap. There was a brief, panting struggle for the gun, then McBride got it and put a knee in the guy's stomach. "Be nice, punk!"

Swiggart loomed over him. "What the hell?"

"By me," McBride said. "Light a match, will you?" He looked down as flame lit the face below him. It was the guard from the dam; the guy McBride had talked to yesterday. His eyes were crazy as he looked at Swiggart. "I'll get you, you murderer!"

Swiggart said, "Oh, yeah? You and who else?"

The guy under McBride tried to wriggle free. McBride put both knees in his stomach. "Take it easy, baby. What's the idea?"

"I—had a—brother in that—tunnel!" the guy gasped.

"Well," McBride said in a reasoning tone, "murder isn't going to help your brother any."

Swiggart, suddenly quite sober, said, "Why, the dirty rat! As if I had anything to do with—"

"Shut up!" McBride said sharply. The door above them had opened, shedding light down the steps. It didn't quite reach the three men in the area. Somebody said, "I don't see anything," and the door banged shut. McBride put his face down close to the guard's. "Look, punk, I'm not going to turn you in for this. Just watch your step, see?" He stood up.

Swiggart booted the prone man in the ribs. McBride's eyes flamed. "Damn it, Swiggart, I said it was finished!" He broke the gun, ejected the shells and threw them far out in the street. He skidded the gun down the sidewalk in the other direction. "Come on, let's get out of here." The guy on the ground was sobbing his heart out. McBride and Swiggart walked swiftly away. On the next street over they caught a cab and Swiggart gave the driver an address. Out of the corners of his eyes he studied McBride's brooding profile. After a while he said, "Well, pal, I guess I owe you something for that."

"Forget it."

"What'd you say your name was?"

"McBride."

They rode in silence for another couple of blocks. The cab pulled up before a third-rate bungalow court. Swiggart, paying off, peeled a bill from a roll big enough to choke a horse. McBride's eyes got a hot, eager light in them. He followed Swiggart down the walk and up the steps of the third unit on the left. Swiggart let himself in with a key.

McBride looked around. The room smelled of incense and there were a lot of gaudy batik cushions. On the mantel over the imitation fireplace there were four or five hand-tinted photos of the same girl.

"Your sister?" McBride asked.

Swiggart leered. "Do I look like a Mexican?" He lifted his voice. "Hey, Nita!"

There was no answer. "She must be out somewhere," Swiggart muttered. He threw his hat and coat on the davenport, went out to the kitchen. McBride could hear glasses rattling. McBride took off his coat and hat, too. When Swiggart came back with a loaded tray McBride had a gun in his fist. He pointed it at Swiggart's fat middle. "Sit down, pal."

THE GUY almost dropped the tray. "Hey, what's the idea?"

"The idea," McBride said, "is for you to sit down before I blow you down. We were going to have a talk, remember?"

"Well, sure, but—" The stupid look went out of his eyes. "Hey, you can't do this to me!"

McBride took two swift, light steps forward, like a dancer, and smacked the flat of the gun against Swiggart's cheek. The tray crashed to the floor. "Who gave you that roll you're carrying?"

Swiggart bent as though to pick up the gurgling bottle, came up inside McBride's guard and smashed a hard right to the heart. McBride gagged, went over backward, and his foot, coming up, caught Swiggart in the stomach. All the color went out of Swiggart's face and he sat down suddenly. McBride crawled on top of him, began beating him over the head with the gun. Neither man was able to talk for a full minute. McBride got his breath back first. "Talk! Who gave you that dough?"

Swiggart heaved under him, rolling his head to avoid the pound of the gun. "I won it!"

"You're a liar," McBride grunted. "You got it for blowing up that tunnel. Who gave it to you?"

Swiggart's suddenly upthrust knee caught McBride in the groin, sent white-hot agony clear up to the top of his head. For a moment all he could think of was to hang onto the gun. He didn't realize that he'd pulled the trigger till he saw that Swiggart was on his feet, on a foot, rather, with the other poised in midair. Then he saw that he'd blown the heel off Swiggart's left shoe, and realized that the roaring in his ears was the echo of the shot. Swiggart put his left foot down slowly, tentatively, not sure that he still had it. His face was the color of dried putty. "Look," he gasped, "look, what that guy said back there, that was all hogwash. The board of inquiry cleared me, didn't they?"

McBride pushed himself erect. "They didn't know how to make a guy talk. I do." He put the gun in his pocket and slugged Swiggart in the mouth. "Come on, baby, sing. Who paid you to do it?"

Swiggart launched a vicious kick. McBride caught his foot, upended him, returned the kick with interest and much better aim. Swiggart yelled. The door behind McBride banged open and Lieutenant Harry Beale plunged in. He had another dick with him. Behind them the courtyard was filled with tenants from the other units. McBride stepped away from Swiggart, straightening his tie.

Beale glared at him. "You again! Hell's fire, McBride, it's getting so that whenever the phone rings—" He swung around. "Close that door!" he yelled.

By this time Swiggart had got to his feet. His eyes were small and hot and murderous. He called McBride a dirty name. McBride pretended to be looking at Beale, but he was really seeing Swiggart's chin, and he brought his right fist up from just above his knee and smacked Swiggart with a very satisfying sound. Swiggart's body described a perfect back layout and clunked to the floor. He didn't move. McBride looked at Beale. "You heard what he called me, didn't you?"

Beale's mouth opened and closed like a gasping fish. "Somebody said there was a shot!" He sniffed. "There was, too. I smell it!"

"Sure," McBride said. "He tried to kill me." He looked at the framed photos of the girl on the mantel. "How did I know she was two-timing him?"

Beale looked at the photos, at McBride, at the unconscious Swiggart. "Well, I'll be—"

"Me too," McBride said. He picked up his hat and coat. "Well, I guess this'll teach him a lesson. If you can forget it I can."

Beale hesitated, trying to catch up with what was going on. Then:

"You mean you don't want to swear out a complaint?"

"How can I," McBride asked reasonably, "without sullying the lady's good name?" He sighed. "Let's get out of here."

They went out. Beale and the other dick rode McBride downtown in the squad car. Under the marquee of the Grand National he said good night and thanked them for coming to his assistance. He went inside. The stewardess from the Los Angeles-Salt Lake plane was sitting in the lobby.

CHAPTER X

REPORT ON AN ADVENTURESS

McBRIDE THOUGHT MAYBE it was an accident. He thought maybe she was waiting for someone else. He tried very hard to think this as he headed for the desk, but it didn't do any good. She waved at him. Sighing, he went over. "Well," he said, "this is a surprise!"

She still wore her uniform, though this was partially concealed by her heavy coat. The jaunty little overseas cap was missing. A small overnight bag was at her feet. She lifted gray eyes to his very dark ones. "You're laughing at me, aren't you?" A slow flush of embarrassment crept up from her throat.

"No, I don't feel much like laughing," he said.

She stood up. The top of her head came to just below his chin. She kept her eyes fixed on the knot of his tie and her voice sounded muffled, as though she were actually in his arms. "I don't know—perhaps it was your flowers, or maybe it was just you. Anyway, you said you'd be riding back with me last night, and then you didn't come. There was the mixup in the names, too. You'd ridden once under a name other than your own. And I remembered your asking about Mr. Train and Mr. Van."

He said gently, "So what did you do, hon?"

She lifted her eyes, dropped them to his tie again. He was glad, for her sake, that the lobby was almost empty. "I found out you were a detective. Some of our own men knew you. I was—"

"Worried about me, hon?"

She wouldn't look at him. "I called your number and there was no answer. That was this evening, when I got back to Los Angeles. So I went out there." She drew an unsteady breath. "There was a woman searching your apartment."

"There was!" He thought rapidly. "Look, was she a black-haired, blue-eyed dame that looked like a million dollars in her clothes?"

She nodded. "I saw her through the window before I rang the bell. She had a gun. But when she let me in the gun had disappeared and she pretended she was waiting for you." There was another quivery intake of breath. "I didn't know what to do. Something might have happened to you. On the other hand, maybe I was interfering in something you had planned. I went away. Then I got to thinking that possibly you had come back here by train and I arranged for a substitute and deadheaded to Palos Verde. And here I am."

"Yes," he said, "and here you are." He put a hand under her chin, tilting her head back. "Look, kitten, do you realize that I don't even know your name?"

She colored. "It's Hope Sullivan."

"Okay, Hope, I'll be back in a minute." He looked at his watch. It was after one in the morning. There was nothing to do but get her a room. He crossed to the desk. "I want a room for Miss Sullivan."

The clerk looked at him. "Near yours, Mr. McBride?"

McBride leaned across the desk. "One more crack like that and I'll kick your teeth in. This girl is a good kid and I don't want you to even look as though she wasn't. Put the room and anything else she gets on my bill."

"Yes, Mr. McBride."

McBride went back to the girl. "You'll have to register, hon. We'll have your bag sent up and then we'll have something to eat. I want to talk to you." She followed him to the desk. The clerk was very polite. Hope Sullivan could have been visiting royalty. McBride led her into the grill and they were shown to a booth. The place was fairly well crowded, noisy enough and busy enough so that McBride and the girl went unremarked.

McBride put his elbows on the table. "I want to tell you about a guy, Hope. And when I'm through I want you to go to your room and forget him. Listening?"

Her clear eyes met his, embarrassed but unafraid. "Yes, McBride, I'm listening. I asked for it, I guess."

He flushed darkly. "I'm ten years older than you are, hon. I know what I'm talking about. This guy is a heel, see? Not the romantic kind of heel, but the gutter kind. He was born in a gutter and he'll probably die in one. The only piece of heart he's got left belongs to someone else—a girl who looks a great deal like you, incidentally. He claims he loves her, but do you think for one minute that this guy plays the game? He doesn't. He chases everything in skirts he sees. You deserve the best, kitten. This guy hasn't got it to give. Understand?"

"Yes," she said, very low, "I understand. Thanks for telling me, McBride." She stood up.

McBride stood up too, and there was Sheila Mason, almost at his elbow. He was too upset to feel any great surprise over her being there; he just knew that she looked quiet and competent, and that her gray eyes were looking from him to the Sullivan girl without rancor. Unshed tears glistened on the Sullivan kid's lashes and she groped unseeingly for her coat. McBride looked at Sheila. "Take her up to her room, will you?" He had to grope a little bit, himself, finding the bar.

HIS REFLECTION in the back bar mirror wore an outraged expression. The bartender swiped a bar towel under his nose. "What happened to the other guy?"

"What other guy?"

"The one that mopped the floor up with you."

For the first time McBride noticed that he did look somewhat rumpled and dirty around the edges. He said, "I must have fallen in a manhole." He pushed his glass across the bar. "Rye."

The cashier from the grill came through the connecting arch. "You forgot to sign the check, Mr. McBride."

He signed it. He hauled a red leather and chromium stool up and sat on it, elbows on the bar, brooding over his drink. Three or four couples came in and one of the men began dropping nickels in the mechanical victrola. This reminded McBride of the guy Swiggart. He thought he'd better go back and finish the job he'd started on Swiggart. Then he decided that probably Swiggart wouldn't be there any more. He straightened as another thought hit him with the effect of a kick in the stomach. If Swiggart really knew something, if he were actually guilty, as the roll of big money indicated, then he would hot-foot it back to the guys who hired him and tell them about McBride. This would do McBride little or no good. It was liable, in fact, to make things just a bit tougher than they were already. Well, it was too late to do anything about it now.

He looked cautiously at the mirror. There was nobody behind him yet, anyway. That was something. He sipped his rye and considered the piece of unexpected information about Miss Ford. There was no doubt in his mind that it had been the lovely and capable Miss Ford whom the little stewardess had caught searching his, McBride's, apartment. Well, she was certainly welcome to anything she got there. The point was, what had she expected to find? McBride gave this one up too, until such time as he could see Miss Ford personally. This was a lead, though. He mustn't forget it.

The thought of that poor Sullivan kid appalled him. A terrible thing to tell a girl she was out of luck, especially after she'd gone to a lot of trouble to find out whether you were alive or dead. This brought him smack up against Sheila's arrival. Now what was Sheila doing in Palos Verde?

A musical voice at McBride's elbow said, "Hello, gambler." McBride shivered. He didn't have to turn, or even to look in the mirror to know who it was. That guy! A fine time for him, of all people, to be coming around. He moved his chin slightly. "Hello, Train."

The gray man was in white tie and tails now, but he was still the gray man to McBride. The color of his hair, his skin, his neat mustache hadn't changed. His eyes hadn't changed either. They still played xylophone tunes on your backbone. McBride knocked over his drink, getting up.

"That's too bad," Train said. "Have another?"

McBride didn't want it, but he said he would have another. The bartender served them. Train spun a silver dollar on the bar. "Match for it?"

McBride watched the dollar with fascinated eyes. "Heads." It came tails. Train put his dollar away. McBride paid for the drink. His hand shook a little as he picked up his glass. "Turning colder, isn't it?"

"I hadn't noticed," Train said. He finished his sherry and bitters, nodded slightly in acknowledgment, went out as quietly as he had come in. McBride crossed the lobby and asked if a wire had come in for him. None had. He went up to his room. He was changing his shirt when there was a knock on the door. "Come in," he said.

IT WAS Sheila. She was wearing business tweeds under a light tweed topcoat. The tweeds were more or less a habit with her. Strangely enough they seemed to enhance rather than detract from her desirability. Sheila wasn't fluffy but she was beautiful.

McBride poked a remnant of shirttail in the top of his pants. "Thanks for taking care of the kid. How is she?"

"She'll be all right. I had quite a talk with her." Sheila moved over to the dresser, took a cigarette, found a chair. "That was a rather nice thing you did, Rex."

"Yeah, a fine thing. A dirty rotten trick, if you ask me, but it had to be done." He turned savage eyes on her. "You talk like I made a great sacrifice or something."

Sheila's eyes stopped him. "Must we always be nasty, Rex? What you did had to be done, of course. She's a nice kid. But you didn't have to make yourself out such a rotten heel."

"Why not? I am one."

"Are you, Rex?"

He looked at her and put a hand up to his cheek, remembering. She said, "I know, I'm sorry I did that, Rex. I was stunned, I guess. For a moment I forgot the many nice things you've done."

He grinned suddenly. "What is this, a peace offering? By the way, what brings you to our unfair city?"

"I had some papers for Colin Leeds to sign."

"The mails stopped running?"

She colored faintly, but her fine gray eyes met his with perfect composure. She tamped out her cigarette. "I also wanted to tell you that I've finally made up my mind. I'll marry you tomorrow, Rex."

He took two swift steps forward, bent over her. His eyes were like a man's who finds water after a week in the Mojave. And then a little devil inside him said, "This is a gag. Even if she means it she isn't doing it for me." He straightened. "What's the deal, Sheila?" He laughed harshly. "McBride saves Leeds & Leeds, gets girl!"

"I don't give a whoop about Leeds & Leeds," she said quietly. "My problem is you. I haven't solved it one way so I'll try the other."

He stared at her suspiciously. "No strings?"

"No strings, Rex." She stood up and he put his arms around her. "That's the nicest thing that has ever happened to me, Sheila." Neither said anything more for a moment or two. Then he pushed her away, kissed her lightly. "We'll have to postpone the big event for a few days, though. I've some things to take care of first."

She looked at him. "What things, Rex?"

He made a great business of putting on his coat and vest. "Just some things. You wouldn't be interested."

"Rex, you're not—?" Whatever she had intended to ask was interrupted by another knock on the door. McBride opened it.

Chief of Police Beale stomped in. He paused abruptly at sight of Sheila. "Oh, so you got company!"

"And what company, Bealsie," McBride said.

Chief Beale looked at everything in the room except McBride. He had the air of a hound with a treed coon. "The lady been here long?"

McBride scowled. "You trying to put the bug on the lady or on me?"

Beale took off his hat. His ball-bearing eyes finally met McBride's head-on. "You had a row with a guy named Swiggart tonight. Right?"

"Right."

"And you later went back and shot him dead."

McBride sucked air into his lungs. "That's a large order for you to prove, Bealsie. Your own brother brought me back to the hotel. I can account for every minute of my time since then. Every minute, get it?"

Beale addressed Sheila directly instead of by inference. "How long you been here with him?"

She looked at her watch. "About fifteen minutes."

You could almost hear Beale calculating. Finally he went to the phone. "Gimme Harry." After a short interval he said, "I got fifteen minutes up here, Harry. How about you?" He hung up discouragedly. "I guess that lets you out, McBride. You couldn't have done it, not even if you was Houdini."

"Thanks, pal, you certainly relieve my mind." McBride was wondering if the crazy guard had let Swiggart have it, or if someone had just closed a mouth that might have become talkative. There was a third possibility. Swiggart might have been knocked over for the roll he carried. He put alert eyes on Beale's red face. "Where'd you pick the guy up?"

"Seventh and San Pedro."

"He have a roll on him? He had when I saw him last."

Beale's eyes shifted. Finally he said, "Well, yes, come to think of it, he did."

"Fine," McBride said approvingly. "There's nothing I admire more than an honest copper. Besides, I can identify the dough."

Beale looked startled. "You can?"

"You bet," McBride lied. He thought of something else. "By the way, I forgot to give your brother the rod I took away from Swiggart. It's had a couple of shots fired. If I were you I'd check it with any slugs you've found lying around loose lately." He went into the bathroom and closed the door and got his own gun out of the flush tank. He had a little trouble drying it. When he came out he was sweating. "There you are, Bealsie."

CHAPTER XI

THE HOURS BEFORE DAWN

IT WAS AROUND two-thirty when McBride got down to Headquarters. It looked cleaner under artificial light, and there was a lot of activity. Cops bustled in and out, and from the tanks at the end of the long stone corridor there was the sound of brawling. The night's quota of drunks, McBride guessed. There was a new desk sergeant on duty, though it looked as though he'd fallen heir to his predecessor's cigar. The sergeant was keeping a pair of phones red hot.

McBride knocked on Chief Beale's door. Lieutenant Harry Beale opened it. Fat lips pointed the quill toothpick accusingly at McBride. "Oh, it's you again!"

McBride made no attempt to deny this. His eyes went past pudgy Harry to the chief at the desk. The chief looked harried. Beyond the chief, lean and tall against the windows, stood Mr. Carmichael, of the Five Companies. His close-set dark eyes surveyed McBride with something that could have been admiration. He didn't say anything.

McBride went in. "I dropped around to have a look at that dough," he said. "It might give you a lead to Swiggart's killer."

Chief Beale managed to look embarrassed. "Well, now, about that dough, McBride—" He looked helplessly at his brother. "You tell him, Harry."

Harry Beale sat creakingly in a swivel chair. "The dough's gone," he said without inflection. It was a statement of fact, flat, brooking no argument. "Somebody lifted it."

"You did," McBride said.

Harry Beale got out of the chair. He moved ponderously until his toes touched McBride's. He removed his toothpick, looked at it, put it back in his mouth. He then attempted to hit McBride in the eye. McBride hit him instead. Beale's eyes crossed and he sat down on the floor. His moon face looked stupid, uncertain. McBride turned humid eyes on the chief. "I warned him this afternoon. I don't care if it is your office, the guy can't pull the same gag on me twice."

The chief looked down at his hulking brother. "You shouldn't ought to have done that, Harry."

Monotonous obscenities dribbled from between Harry's thick lips. "He said I stole the dough, didn't he?"

All this time Carmichael hadn't moved from his position by the windows, hadn't said a word. From the expression on his face he was a predatory bird waiting to pick the bones. Harry Beale grunted to his feet. The chief said, "Harry didn't take the dough. We don't know who did. It just disappeared from my desk, that's all."

McBride looked at Harry. "In that case, Lieutenant, I apologize. You didn't take the dough."

"You're damned right I didn't!"

"I said you didn't." McBride turned to Carmichael. "Well, how's my new employer? Anybody else been shooting at you?"

"No," Carmichael said. His eyes warmed a little.

Chief Beale cleared his throat noisily. "That's one we owe you, McBride. You know that gun you gave us? Well, we checked it like you said, and you know what? Damned if it wasn't the gun that fired the two slugs through Mr. Carmichael's window!"

McBride pretended to be greatly surprised. "The hell you say!"

"Fact. Swiggart was the guy tried to burn Carmichael. That's why we ain't too worried over who got Swiggart. He had it coming."

"Maybe Carmichael did it," McBride said.

Carmichael's thin lips writhed. "I thought you were working for me."

McBride spread his hands, remembering the false trail he had laid. "We're all friends here, aren't we? What difference does it make?"

Chief Beale glared at him. "I don't like those kind of remarks, McBride. I don't like 'em at all. Besides, Carmichael couldn't have done it. He's proved it."

"I wondered why he was down here," McBride said. He shrugged. "Well what's another unsolved murder to Palos Verde, eh?"

Harry Beale made rumbling noises in his throat. "Another crack like that and we'll pin the job on you."

"You can't," McBride said. "I've got an alibi."

"By the way," Chief Beale said casually, "who was that lady I seen you with tonight?"

McBride leered. "That was no lady. That was—" He broke off as Carmichael snapped his fingers impatiently. "Lay off, McBride. I want to talk to you." He put on his hat, went to the door.

McBride looked at the Beales. "Well, glad to have been able to help you boys out. All you've got to do now is find who took the dough."

Chief Beale's eyes glinted. "That's another thing, McBride. You said you could identify the money. How were you going to do that?"

McBride knew that he had almost tripped himself on that one. If he lied and said he had the serial numbers, they'd ask him for the list. If he gave them a fake list he'd be spotting himself, because he still wasn't sure that the money had ever left this office. Also, he wasn't supposed to have been with Swiggart long enough to have copied down a lot of numbers. He said lamely, "Well, it was just an idea. While we were battling I happened to get hold of the roll for a second. I might have left a print or two."

He thought the Beales looked relieved. Harry said, "Nuts. It might have worked if we still had the dough, but if we still had it we wouldn't need your identification. We took it off the guy."

"But you didn't copy the numbers," McBride said. "That was bad. You'd have traced the guy in no time if you had the numbers." He sighed. "Well, life is like that, I guess. No matter how hard you try you never get any place." He followed the impatient Carmichael out to the street.

THEY walked for a while without saying anything. Grand Avenue was crowded. Neon signs bloomed against the sky like a surrealist painting. Shrill laughter dinned at your ears, tinsel froth topping a sea of unholy smells and sounds. McBride hoped Sheila was asleep.

Carmichael halted before the glare of the Club Natividad. His eyes massaged McBride's face, trying to squeeze information out of it. Finally he said, "You're smarter than I gave you credit for, my friend."

"Is that so?"

"Why should Swiggart have shot at me?"

"By me," McBride said. "You ought to know the reason."

Carmichael looked genuinely puzzled. "That's the hell of it, I don't. The man was practically—" He broke off suddenly.

"A friend of yours?"

"Of course not. Why should you think that?"

"I don't think," McBride said. "I just move around."

Frank admiration showed in Carmichael's eyes. "You do at that, McBride. How you were able to locate the man and kill him and still fool the Beales—well, it's beyond me!"

McBride said, "I didn't kill him."

Carmichael winked. "Of course you didn't. And even if you had I wouldn't expect you to talk about it. Just the same, I think you're going to be a very valuable man to me, McBride. A very, very valuable man. In fact I think we could even stand another fifty a day. *And* expenses."

McBride shrugged. "Money is always useful. By the way, did the Beales say what kind of a gun killed Swiggart?"

"A thirty-eight. Swiggart's rod, the one you took away from him, was a forty-five."

"That ought to prove I had nothing to do with it," McBride said. He managed to look self-conscious. "The permit you wangled for me calls for a twenty-five auto. Besides, I had an alibi."

"Of course." Carmichael's eyes were brilliant in the light. "Of course you did, McBride." He yawned delicately behind a lean brown hand. "Well, see me tomorrow, will you?" He went into the crowded Club Natividad.

McBride moved on up Grand Avenue. He wished he knew who had Swiggart's dough. If either or both of the Beales had it, it could be just plain larceny. If it had really been stolen by someone else, then the someone else was undoubtedly Swiggart's killer and probably Swiggart's unknown employer in the matter of the dynamiting The theft of the dough was proof that it could have been traced back to its source. Then why hadn't the killer taken it off Swiggart at the time of the kill? Because he'd been hurried? Or because he hadn't considered the money a danger until it was called to his attention? Who, incidentally, could have called it to his attention but the Beales? McBride had told no one but the chief that he could identify the money. There was another angle here. It was possible the Beales were shielding the real killer. But if this were so, why had the chief of police tried to pin the job on McBride? Was he supposed to have been the fall guy? Several things made this theory impractical. The chief had been too ready to accept McBride's explanation. True, McBride's alibi was almost airtight, but any hardworking police department could have arranged matters to coincide if they so desired. Maybe Carmichael's obvious influence at Headquarters had pulled the heat off. Still, it had looked as though the Beales had been accusing Carmichael himself of pulling the job. This seemed to indicate the Beales were really ignorant of just who had gunned Swiggart. The money could have been stolen from the desk at Headquarters as the chief claimed. Or the chief could be holding it out.

McBride turned in at the Grand National. Well, the hell with that for a while. The one thing that was capable of being proved immediately was whether or not the crazy-eyed guard had shot Swiggart. The gun McBride had taken away from him, there in the area beside the house on B Street, was the same caliber, a thirty-eight. The guy might have picked it up, got some more cartridges and found Swiggart a second time. McBride didn't really think this. He just had to be sure. The old process of elimination again. He hoped he wouldn't be eliminated, like Swiggart. He hoped that he would live a long, long time. He was optimistic rather than otherwise about the apparent stalemate in the Swiggart case. No matter what happened, he, McBride, had certainly built himself a reputation with Carmichael. This might possibly lead to an assignment that would prove something.

THERE was still no wire at the desk for him. Well, you could hardly expect a stock broker to be awake at three in the morning, McBride thought. He went into a phone booth and called the timekeeper's office at the dam. "You've got a guy working the day shift in guard tower 5. He had a brother in that tunnel accident."

"You mean Smitty?"

McBride said he didn't know whether he meant Smitty or not. He described the guard. "That's Smitty, all right," the guy at the other end said. "Frank Smith. His brother's name was Joe."

"Is he around?" McBride asked. "Not Joe—Frank."

"Just a minute, I'll look it up." There was a wait of several minutes. McBride had to drop another quarter in the coin box. The voice returned. "Why, Frank asked for a leave of absence. He isn't off the payroll, he just checked out for a few days. He was pretty busted up over his brother. I think maybe you could find him at his brother's place. Joe was married."

McBride said he hadn't known. He thanked his informant for telling him, though. He said, "Would you have the wife's address?" After another short wait he got this too. He went out and got in a cab.

The house was not much to look at. It was a dumpy little box of a place in a whole row of the same kind. Discouraged looking lawns fronted the street, separated by stunted geranium hedges. If the rents were over twenty dollars a month the tenants were being robbed. There were lights in some of the houses, none in the one McBride wanted. He went up the short walk, tried the sagging steps gingerly, found they would hold him and mounted to the porch. He had to ring three or four times before a light finally went on inside.

Frank Smith opened the door. "What's the idea?"

McBride pushed his hat back on his head. "Remember me, Smitty?"

Smith tried to slam the door and McBride stuck his foot in it. "Now don't go temperamental on me, Smitty. I just want to talk to you."

Smith let go of the door and ran into the room at his left. McBride ran after him. He almost ran smack into a dose of lead. Smith's eyes were crazy again and he had a gun. "Get out, you heel!"

From another room a woman's voice called, "What is it, Frank?"

This guy Smith couldn't seem to talk to anybody unless he was looking in their direction. He moved his eyes from McBride toward the sound of the woman's voice, saying, "Nothing, Lou. Go back to sleep," and he was very surprised when McBride's fist closed over the gun cylinder. He kept trying to pull the trigger, but without result because McBride was much the stronger. Fear climbed into his eyes and he lashed out with his left. McBride imprisoned that too.

"Now," he said quietly, "let's talk."

The woman called, "Frank, is it about Joe?"

"Tell her no," McBride said. "It is, but we don't want to worry her any more, do we?"

Smith's hand fell away from the gun. "No, Lou. Everything's all right. Go back to sleep. Take another one of those pills the doctor left." He sat down weakly, hopelessly, staring at McBride with lackluster eyes. "What do you want? Why couldn't you have let me kill that guy?"

"Because they'd have hung you for it," McBride said. "Besides, I wanted to talk to the guy." He broke the gun. It was loaded full up. He smelled the barrel. It hadn't been cleaned; it still smelled of burned cordite. "I see you got some more slugs, Smitty."

"Sure. So what?"

"Where'd you go after we left you?"

Smith's shoulders drooped. "I came home." He seemed to be struggling with an elusive thought. "I don't know, you knocked hell out of me when you fell off that porch. Some of the craziness went away. I got to thinking you could identify me if anything happened to Swiggart, so I—I just came home."

McBride thought that probably this was exactly what had happened. Nobody in his right mind would fumble an attempt at murder, be recognized by a third party and go right out and try it again. To do a good job of it he'd have to kill the witness too. The only thing was, you couldn't be sure Smith had been in his right mind. He'd had that same crazy look no more than two minutes ago when he'd tried to shoot McBride.

"Why'd you try to smoke me just now, Smitty?"

"You're a friend of the guy's, aren't you? I've been expecting you and him to look me up most any time." He wet his lips. "Go on, get it over with."

McBride nodded, almost satisfied. He tried a last test. "Ever hear of ballistics, Smitty? They can match a gun with the slugs fired from it just as easy as shooting fish."

"They don't even have to look for the slug I shot," Smith said resignedly. "I'll admit I fired it. I wish it had killed him."

"Thank you," McBride said. He tossed the gun in a corner, turned toward the door. Over his shoulder he said, "It was tough on me, Smitty, but somebody sure did you a big favor. Swiggart is dead."

Smith got up slowly. "Say that again."

"Somebody tagged your pal Swiggart. For keeps."

Smith's mouth curled derisively. "And you thought I did it!" He began to laugh.

McBride slapped him across the mouth. "Stop that, you fool. You'll wake her up!"

Smith ran the back of his hand over a suddenly moist forehead. "Yeah, yeah, you're right." He stared at McBride as though really seeing him for the first time. "Hey, was it you gave it to him? You were with him when—"

"Don't mention it," McBride said. "Don't ever mention it to anybody. It happens that I didn't kill the guy, but there are mugs in this town that would grab at anything to help pin it on me. It's bad enough as it is. I was caught beating him once, but that was supposed to be over a dame. If they find out I actually went into that dive after him—"

"Don't worry about me," Smith said. "I'd go to hell for the guy that did it."

McBride laughed shortly.

"Well, that's more than I would, pal. I'm sore about it, myself. Not that he didn't have it coming, but I've learned that you can't find out a thing from a dead guy. Look, did you really have something on this mug, or were you just crazy enough to pick the only target in sight?"

Smith licked his lips. "Swiggart hated my brother. I thought that—"

McBride cursed quietly. Every time he thought he had something a new angle popped up. This time it was a small time personal feud. "Not even Swiggart would have killed them all to get one, you dope. Sure you don't know of something else?"

"No. It—well, it seemed reasonable to me at the time. And the board of inquiry exonerating him and all—"

McBride sighed. "Okay, Smitty, forget it." He went out to his cab and back to the hotel and went to bed. It was almost dawn.

CHAPTER XII

FINGERS TAPPING

McBRIDE AWAKENED TO find rain beating against his windows and at first he thought that this was what had roused him. Then he discovered that it was someone knocking quietly on his door. It was scarcely more than a tapping of fingers. "All right," he called, and got up and went across to the door in his bare feet. Silently he removed the chair braced under the knob, as silently turned the key. He then got back into bed and pulled the blankets up to his chin. Under the covers his gun pointed steadily at the door. "Come in."

He felt silly when his caller turned out to be Sheila Mason. He scowled. "Trying to compromise me, hunh?"

She was dressed, even to topcoat and hat, and she carried her tooled leather briefcase. "I'm checking out, Rex. Is there anything you wanted to say to me?"

He avoided her eyes. "What about the Sullivan kid—the stewardess?"

"We're going back on the same plane."

"Fine," he said, yawning. "That's swell."

Sheila came over and sat on the edge of the bed. "Rex, you're playing a dangerous game up here."

He yawned again. "Compared with me, hon, a child chess prodigy with forty adult opponents has got nothing on his mind. How's about a kiss?"

She shook her head. "Why are you doing it, Rex? Whose side are you on, really?"

"My own. If I don't get some dough out of this it'll be because I'm dead or the government has quit making it."

Her gray eyes darkened. "You said you'd quit if I married you. Remember?"

"Could I ever forget it?" He touched his cheek as if the marks of her fingers were still there. And then, seeing her frown: "All right, I made you an offer and you turned it down. Now you're ready to take me up on it. Can I help it if something has come up in the meantime that makes quitting an impossibility? You've made me wait around for a couple years. Surely you can wait for a day or two."

She studied him. "If I just knew, Rex. It's the uncertainty that gets you."

He sat up suddenly, angrily, and the movement exposed his gun. Sheila saw it. Her fine hands balled into fists. "Rex, here you are lying in bed with a gun pointed at the door and you expect me not to worry."

"How about me?" he yelled. "Your coming here at this time, being seen with me for even a moment, is enough to drive a guy screwy. Somebody gets the notion I'm nuts about you they'll have a swell club in their hands. Go back to Los. Stay there. Keep out from under my feet!"

Sheila stood up. "Very well, Rex." She went to the door.

He said, "Hey, how's about that kiss?"

She came back and bent over him. Her lips were cold. "Goodbye, Rex." Then she was gone. He stared at the closed door for a long moment. "Goodbye, hon," he said in a curiously gentle voice. He rolled over and buried his face in the pillows.

After a while he looked at his watch, saw that it was nine o'clock, decided that what he needed was a hot tub. He didn't know why he was so depressed. Possibly it was the rain driving down out of leaden skies. He had made some progress in the case; not much, but some. He had proved, at least to his own satisfaction, that the man Swiggart was in some measure re-

sponsible for the explosion in Diversion Tunnel 3. Whoever
had hired Swiggart had killed him to close his mouth. True,
Swiggart was beyond reach now, but there must be other guys
like him. Besides, McBride still had one more lead to follow
up in the matter of Swiggart. Also, if the news got around that
Swiggart had been in contact with McBride, it might be
assumed that Swiggart had already talked. This should make
someone very nervous indeed, and a nervous man is frequent-
ly a careless man.

McBride soaked in the tub. Eyes closed, body relaxed, he
considered his new status with Mr. Carmichael, and Carmichael's in relation to the brothers Beale. A gun permit had been
issued to McBride on Carmichael's recommendation. Boiled
down, this was all it amounted to. Any citizen affiliated with
as important an outfit as the Five Companies could have done
as much. There seemed to be some sort of an undercurrent
which hinted at more than this, but McBride couldn't put a
finger on it.

Shaving, he regarded his reflection in the mirror without
admiration. He kept seeing two faces beside his own: Sheila's
and Miss Ford's. He couldn't make up his mind which he liked
best this morning. His eyes glowed briefly, remembering Miss
Ford. He must look her up again one of these days, especially
if something tangible didn't break here in Palos Verde. Miss
Ford with a gun, and searching his, McBride's, apartment,
became a more charming enigma than ever. He must certainly
make a point of seeing Miss Ford.

Yes, definitely.

HE DRESSED and went down and consumed a moderate
breakfast. Over his second cup of coffee he read the morning
paper. Apparently no further mishaps had occurred at the dam.
McBride sighed relievedly. There was about a stick and a half
covering the shooting of Swiggart. No motive for the job was
offered. Swiggart, being dead, was unable to defend himself
against the allegation that it had been he who fired the myste-

rious shots through Mr. Carmichael's window. In this instance, however, an excellent motive had been brought to light. Swiggart had once been discharged from a Five Companies job by none other than Mr. Carmichael. Presumably he had been sore about it.

McBride nodded approvingly. Neat but not gaudy. He hoped that everything he did would find as ready an explanation. A bell-hop came through the dining room, paging Mr. McBride. He had a yellow envelope on a silver salver. McBride exchanged a quarter for the envelope, opened it. The wire was the one he had been expecting. It said, "Yes," and followed this laconic observation with a list of abbreviations indicating that a certain party had made a lot of money in the market recently. McBride put the envelope in his pocket. He wished the wire had said no instead of yes, because now he would have to concentrate on the gray man, and even the thought of the gray man gave him goose pimples.

He was so interested in analyzing his feelings about Train that he wasn't conscious of the new menace bearing down on him until Mr. Erin Rourke was actually at his table. The roundish, roly-poly little vice president of Acme Indemnity was his usual volatile self. He was, he said, very glad to see McBride. He said it again: "I'm certainly glad to see you!"

"The pleasure is all yours," McBride said.

Rourke was hurt. He looked like a slightly mature cherub. His Cupid's-bow mouth drooped. "Is that nice, McBride? Haven't I always been your friend? Who was it that stood up on his hind legs and defended you before Franz Charles and the others?"

"Good old Rourke," McBride said. "The peepul's pal."

Rourke pulled out a chair. He was without hat or topcoat, so presumably he was registered here. He examined the menu. "Steak," he finally decided. He lifted a pudgy forefinger for a waiter. "The filet, blood rare. With mushrooms."

McBride shuddered. "For breakfast?"

Rourke beamed. "Nothing like a good meal to start the day off right." He unfolded his napkin, spread it over his paunch. "Yes, sir, too many men of my age make the mistake of dieting. Now me, I always say—"

"Too much," McBride scowled. He started to get up, thought better of it. "Now look, if you've got any idea you can come up here and talk me into changing my mind about resigning—"

Rourke lifted a hand. "Have I ever tried to change your mind? Have I ever tried to change anybody's? Trouble with me is I'm too easy-going. I let people walk all over me, that's what I do. Not," he added complacently, "that I don't know a good man when I see one. I've got a job for you, McBride."

McBride stared. "You mean you came all the way up here to hire me?"

Rourke's steak was rare all right. A hunk of it on his poised fork dripped red. "Well, yes and no. Sort of two birds with one stone, if you get what I mean. My wife is up here getting a divorce and I dropped around to see if she had enough money. Fine woman, my wife. Excellent woman."

"So you're financing her divorce," McBride said dryly.

Rourke beamed. "Why not? I financed the wedding, didn't I?"

There seemed to be no answer to this logic. McBride returned to the proffered job. "What kind of a job is it?"

Rourke pursed his lips. "Straight fraud case. Only thing is, you'd have to go to New York. You tied up here?"

"Nothing I couldn't leave. What's in it for me?"

"A couple grand?"

McBride shook his head. "Unh-unh."

Rourke munched his steak. After a while he said, "Five?" He didn't look at McBride. He was examining with great interest an oil on the far wall depicting the beauties of the Grand Canyon. He waved his fork. "Nice piece, that."

McBride said, "No."

"The Grand Canyon?" Rourke brought his eyes around slowly. "Oh, you mean the five grand offer. Well, maybe—"

"Never mind," McBride said. "You've already offered too much. Any fraud job worth five grand to you isn't a fraud. It's a frame. I don't want any part of it."

Rourke shrugged plump shoulders. "Okay, I was just giving you a chance. You going moral on us, McBride?"

"I'm walking out on you," McBride said. He got up. "Just like I did on the Alliance." He started off, turned and came back. "And don't bother looking me up with any more of your screwy offers."

Rourke laid his knife and fork down carefully. "You may be sorry for that, McBride."

"Is that a threat?"

"Don't be silly, boy. What could I threaten you with?"

"You could blackball me in L.A."

Rourke was anguished. "Would I do that? I ask you, would I?" He let his shoulders droop pathetically. "Haven't we always been friends, Rex?"

"That's the trouble," McBride said. "A guy can take care of his enemies. Friends are just a plain nuisance." He put a hand on Rourke's shoulder, to partly take the sting out of his words. "You're not a bad guy, Erin. For a crook." He went out to the lobby.

A GUY wearing a chauffeur's cap got out of a chair. McBride didn't recognize him till he removed the cap. Then he saw that it was Engstrom, the alleged murderer of the hardware salesman. The marks of Harry Beale's fists were still plain on the guy's face, but he looked better than when McBride had seen him last. He spoke from the corner of his mouth. "See you a minute, Mr. McBride?"

"Sure."

Engstrom twisted the cap in his hands. "Well, look, I owe

you plenty for helping to spring me from under that rap. Anything I can do—"

"Forget it," McBride said.

"In a pig's eye I'll forget it." McBride got the impression that Engstrom was thinking of the Beales. Engstrom was a small guy but he looked like a good hater. He said, "Palos Verde is a tough town if you don't know your way around."

"Or even if you do," McBride conceded. "Look at what happened to you."

Engstrom's good eye glowed. The other was still puffy, slitted, giving him a very evil appearance indeed. "What I'm trying to tell you, pal, is that I've got a hack. You'd be safer riding with me than with some of the others."

"Oh, drumming up business, hunh?"

Engstrom's skin, where it wasn't blue and purple, turned brick-colored. "Don't tell me you're just another heel. I'm trying to steer you right."

McBride considered. This guy might be useful at that. He knew the town. He'd been in business here. Besides, while it wasn't a certainty, it was possible the guy might be as grateful as he sounded. McBride looked out at Grand Avenue. It was still raining cats and dogs. "Okay," he said, "I was just going to call a cab anyway. You might as well make the dough." He followed Engstrom out to the hack. They rode across town to the court McBride had visited the night before with Swiggart.

Engstrom got out, opening an umbrella. "Well, thanks pal," McBride said. "You certainly do give service." He sloshed up the walk, rang the bell of the third unit on the left. He had to ring three or four times before he got an answer. Then it wasn't the door that opened. It was half of one of the French windows. The gal who looked out at him was the one whose pictures decorated the mantel over the imitation fireplace. She was wearing pajamas and a flame-colored corduroy robe. She was not in the best of humor.

"W'at you want, hanh?"

"You, *chiquita*," McBride said gallantly. "I dropped in last night and saw your pictures."

Her eyes were like a cat's. "You were 'ere weeth Swiggart?"

"Unh-hunh."

She vanished from the window, reappeared at the door. "Come in."

He went in, past her, occupied with folding the umbrella. Some sixth sense made him turn and he caught the flash of light on descending steel. He almost broke her wrist with the umbrella. The knife clattered to the floor. "Well," he said. He was breathing gustily, as though he'd been running. "Well!"

She snarled at him, baring small white teeth. Her brown skin had turned the color of old parchment. "You keel heem!"

He examined Engstrom's umbrella. It seemed to be all right. "Sure," he said casually. "I think I'll kill you too."

She plunged down after the knife, but her right wrist was still numb and this made her clumsy. McBride had no trouble disarming her. Pinning her slight body to him with his left arm he looked down at the knife in his other hand. It was a cute little thing. It looked as Mexican and as vicious as the girl herself. She began to whimper.

He released her suddenly, gave her a slight push and she stumbled backward into the pile of batik cushions on the divan. Her cat eyes hated him. He tested the knife on his thumb. It was sharp enough to shave with. She didn't scream. Perhaps she couldn't scream. She just sat there waiting for what she thought was to come.

McBride put the knife on the mantel. "You little hell-cat."

"Bah!"

Something about the whole thing struck McBride as very funny and he started to laugh. "*Chiquita*, I didn't kill your boy friend. Not that he didn't have it coming. He was cheating on you."

She stared at him. " 'Ow you know thees?"

"The first time I saw the guy he was with a girl in a dive over on B Street. In fact we came from there here, and when I saw your pictures I started to tell him what a heel he was, treating you like that. He got sore and I had to bop him one. But I didn't kill him."

THE GIRL sat up. "Nita," she said, "Nita, she theenk you maybe say true." Her cat eyes probed his face. After a while she said, "The no-good cheater!"

"A fitting epitaph," McBride agreed. "Nice place you've got here, Juanita."

"You like?"

He nodded emphatically. "I like." The sound of the rain outside was like drumfire. McBride teetered on his heels in front of the fake fireplace. He still wore his hat and overcoat. The girl curled up like a kitten among the cushions, watching him. He shivered a little.

She said, "You cold, hanh? You stay, I make fire."

He shook his head. "Sorry, toots, I've got some business to take care of. Tonight?"

She moved lazily among the cushions. "W'y not?"

"What's your racket, *chiquita?*"

"Me, I'm dancer. I dance Club Natividad."

"Van's place, eh?" Van was the enormously fat man who had sat directly in front of McBride on the plane; the one the papers described as a genial host. McBride framed his next question carefully. "That where you met Swiggart?"

"That devil!"

"Well, is it?" McBride persisted.

She was on her feet in one unbroken, lightning-swift movement. "You copper? W'at for you ask Nita all thees theeng?"

McBride leaned on the mantel. "It's only because I like you, kid. I wouldn't want you to get in a jam, see? Take Van now, Van's liable to find himself in a spot 'most any minute, and anybody connected with him is liable to be in a spot too. See what I mean?"

"W'at kind of spot?"

"Well, somebody got to Swiggart, didn't they?" He watched her brown skin turn ivory. "That roll of dough he had was a dead giveaway. He give you any of it?"

He saw immediately that he had struck pay dirt. The way her face tightened up told him. He hauled money out of his pocket. "Better let me trade you some of this for it, babe."

She stared at him. "W'y you do thees for Nita?"

He frowned impatiently. "I told you. It's because I like you. There were fourteen men killed in that tunnel, babe. Think they're going to stop looking beyond Swiggart?"

She gasped. "No! No, I know not'ing about it!"

"Did I say you did?" He watched her from under half-lowered lids. "Swiggart tell you anything about it?"

"That rat!" she said.

After a while he got her to talk a little. Swiggart had gambled at Van's place. He'd lost. He'd even borrowed money from her. Repaying her later from a roll as big as her arm, he'd refused to tell her where he'd got it. She hadn't connected the money and the accident and Swiggart's discharge until just now.

McBride asked, "Swiggart seem pretty close to this guy Van?"

She shrugged. "I don't know."

"Okay, *chiquita*," McBride said after a while, "you let me have the dough Swiggart gave you. Then you can forget the whole thing."

She went into the bedroom. When she came out she was holding two creased hundred-dollar bills by their extreme corners, as if they might be bloody. McBride tried not to snatch them. Here, he felt, was his first real lead. He mustn't do anything to spoil it. His fingers shook a little as he counted out an equivalent amount from his own money. The two bills he put in the fob pocket of his pants. "I wouldn't say anything about this, Juanita."

She looked as though she were going to be sick. He went out hastily. Rain drenched him as he stood on the steps trying to get the umbrella open. It wouldn't open. Cursing, he ran for the cab.

Engstrom said, "For crying out loud, don't you even know how to open an umbrella?"

McBride squeezed water out of his hat. "You open that one and I'll kiss your neck. It's jammed."

Engstrom opened it without the slightest trouble. "See?"

CHAPTER XIII

BOTH ENDS AND THE MIDDLE

MR. CARMICHAEL WAS in his office behind the big plate glass windows with the Venetian blinds. He was wearing a double-breasted blue worsted, black shoes, a black tie. He looked like a rather sinister undertaker. He frowned at McBride. "You're late."

"Could I help it?" McBride demanded resentfully. He was still sore about the umbrella. He stank of wet wool.

Carmichael made a church and steeple of his lean brown hands. His dark, too-close-together eyes examined McBride. "Sit down, my boy. I want to have a talk with you."

McBride didn't sit down. He said he was afraid he'd stick to the chair. He stood with his back to the windows, face in shadow, studying Carmichael covertly. Carmichael shrugged, pushing a full humidor across the desk. McBride lit a cigar. He had to use three matches to do it because even the insides of his pockets were wet.

Carmichael cleared his throat. "It strikes me that you're a cut above the average gunsel, McBride."

"You ought to know," McBride said. "You've probably hired plenty of them."

Carmichael admitted this without batting an eye. "In the construction business there are many things to consider." He flicked ash into a bronze tray, considering his next words carefully. "I hired you in a weak moment, McBride. I admire the way you accomplish things. But now that I've got you I don't exactly know what to do with you. As a bodyguard you seem to spend precious little time with the man you're supposed to be guarding."

McBride said, "Well, what would you suggest?"

"I was about to ask you the same thing, McBride. How do you think you could be valuable to the Five Companies?"

McBride played a tune on his lower lip, thinking. "Well, I wouldn't be much good to you at the dam. I don't know a mixer from a dynamo." He brightened. "Could I knock off Colin Leeds for you?"

Mr. Carmichael was mildly horrified. "How do you think that would help us?"

"Everything that's happening helps you," McBride said. "Leeds & Leeds are certainly building a reputation as stumble-bums. If I'm any judge, the Five Companies ought to get all the big jobs for the next hundred years."

Carmichael got up. Something about the way he did it reminded McBride of the girl Juanita. Not that Carmichael looked Mexican. He just had the same cat-like quality of movement. He stood over McBride, so tall that McBride had to look up at him.

"Do I understand you're accusing us of this sabotage?"

"I never accuse anybody of anything," McBride said. "I merely mentioned it in passing."

"Well, don't mention it again—ever." Carmichael resumed his seat, built a new church and steeple. He stared over this at McBride. "You were originally hired by the Underwriters' Alliance."

McBride blew a smoke ring. "Sure."

"And you quit?"

"What do you think?" McBride said. "Any sniping that's done it's going to be me, not the other guy. I don't like being a target."

"Oh?"

McBride explained how he had arrived in Palos Verde. He thought that probably Mr. Carmichael knew all about it, but he explained anyway. "Too many people knew I was coming up here. Somebody with a gun was expecting me."

"But you fooled them," Carmichael said admiringly.

McBride shrugged. "You know what Abe Lincoln said. Me, I like to be on the winning side."

"Meaning mine?"

"I wouldn't know." McBride lifted one of the slats of the blind, looked out at Engstrom's cab. Engstrom was reading a magazine. It was still raining.

Carmichael drummed nervous fingers on the desk. "The bodyguard business is out, McBride. It just happened to fit at the moment, but Swiggart is dead and the need for it seems to have passed."

"So I'm fired?"

"I wouldn't say that, my boy, I wouldn't say that. The fact of the matter is that we're interested in Leeds & Leeds' operations. Purely from an objective standpoint. As I told you before, we're still learning. Leeds & Leeds' problems will at some time or other be our problems. The more we can find out about how they're solved the more intelligently may we attack our own when they arise. See what I mean?"

"I see what you mean me to see."

Carmichael let this pass. "I would suggest a sort of roving commission, McBride. You may be able to pick up oddments of information here and there. How does that strike you?"

"I like to rove," McBride said. He thought that he was treading on dangerous ground, but he made a suggestion just to see the effect on Carmichael. "I could probably rove right over to Colin Leeds and get the same kind of a job."

Carmichael was delighted. "McBride, that's an idea! You could do it. Probably you've already been approached, eh?" He broke off suddenly. "The only thing is, how would I know—?"

"Which side I was selling out?" McBride grinned. "You've got nothing to lose. You haven't told me anything."

Carmichael was overcome. "You private dicks!" he gasped. "You'll kill me!"

McBride thought this was quite likely. He didn't like Carmichael very well. He said, strengthening his position: "Leeds & Leeds are pressed financially. Train is on the board of one of their banks and I understand he isn't making it any easier for them."

All the joy went out of Mr. Carmichael's lean brown face. "Train, eh?" He looked at McBride. "You'd better lay off Train, fellow. He's bad medicine."

"You're telling me!" McBride put on his soggy hat. "Well, I guess I'll be running along."

"How about dinner tonight?"

"At your house?"

"Yes."

"Maybe I will, at that." McBride went out.

CROSSING the sidewalk he yelled at Engstrom to open the cab door. Engstrom did this, still reading his magazine. McBride looked over his shoulder at the lurid cover. "You'll ruin your eyes reading stuff like that."

"You'd be surprised," Engstrom said, "the realism they get into these things lately. I was just reading about a couple coppers beating up on a guy." He looked at his bruised reflection in the rear-vision mirror. "It was realistic as hell."

McBride sneezed. "I think I'm catching cold. We better go back to the hotel."

"Sure," Engstrom said. They went back to the Grand National. Getting out, McBride looked at the meter. It said he owed Engstrom twelve dollars and forty cents. "Well, blow me down!"

Engstrom said aggrievedly, "Can I help it if you like to talk? Tell you what I'll do. I'll call it twelve dollars even."

McBride said, "And you're the guy that warned me against the other hackers. I wish I'd let 'em hang you." He sneezed violently.

Engstrom said, "By the day, now, it's cheaper."

"How much cheaper?"

"Well, call it forty bucks. And that's a steal."

"You don't have to brag," McBride said. "You charge the twelve off against the forty?"

Engstrom sighed. "Oh, all right. I'm not one to haggle over pennies. When I like a guy I like him."

McBride sneered. "Am I lucky!" He banged through the lobby toward the elevators. The Queen of Diamonds got out of a chair, blocking his path. She looked like a million dollars. She was wearing seal this time. "Hello, Irish."

"Oh, hello!" He got out his handkerchief, made a great business of blowing his nose. "How are you?"

"I thought you were coming back last night."

"Did I say that?"

She lifted a chin at the elevators. "Maybe we could talk more comfortably somewhere else."

"What about?"

Her lips scarcely moved. "About Swiggart. There are guys that might be interested in knowing you came in my place after him."

McBride sneezed again and this made him angry. "Look, toots, if this is a shakedown you can go hang. I didn't kill the lug and the cops proved I didn't."

Her beautiful lips curved downward in a sneer almost as good as one of McBride's. "The cops! A fine bunch of cops we've got in this town. And anyway I'm not talking about who killed the guy. I'm talking about you being interested in him."

"What makes you think I was?"

"I get around, Irish, I get around. I know exactly how much you gave one of my girls to point him out to you; I know that

the brawl afterward wasn't over any *señorita*. What did Swiggart
tell you?"

"Nothing. I didn't ask him anything."

"You're a liar, McBride."

"All right, I'm a liar. Also I'm soaking wet and working up a
swell case of double pneumonia. Whatever it is you're trying
to prove, go ahead and prove it."

"There are some people that don't need proof, McBride. They
play hunches. Believe it or not, I'm trying to do you a good
turn."

"Thanks for nothing."

"All right, just remember that Lou Queen warned you. Somebody else may figure things out the same way I did." She lifted
her head, stared him straight in the eye. "You're a fool, McBride."

He took off his hat. "I guess I am at that, Queen. It's this
cold. Mind if I take a rain check on that date last night?"

She laughed suddenly, musically. "I don't know what I see in
you, Irish. I guess I must like fools. Okay, drop around when
you get time." She swept past him. He thought, "McBride, old
boy, you must be losing your grip. Everybody in town seems to
know more about what you're doing than you do yourself." He
went up to his room, turned on the hot water in the tub, started
shedding his soggy clothes. There was a knock on the door.
McBride, clad only in shorts, picked up his gun and retreated
to the bath. He was shivering. "Come in."

Engstrom came in. He looked at the gun in McBride's fist.
"A fine way to welcome a guy."

McBride said, "This isn't a hotel room. This is the grand
concourse at Santa Anita. It's getting so a guy can't even take
a bath in privacy any more."

Engstrom took the gun out of McBride's hand. "Okay, take
your bath." McBride sank luxuriously into the steaming tub.
Engstrom examined his puffy face in the mirror. "I noticed you
talking to Lou Queen."

McBride slid down until the water covered his chin. "Does the forty a day include chaperonage?"

Engstrom was now using McBride's razor. "I just thought you'd like to know," he said casually. "If it wasn't for Lou I'd still be in the hardware business. Expensive gal, Lou."

CHAPTER XIV

CAUSE AND EFFECTS

HE AWOKE SLOWLY, comfortably, and was surprised to find that he felt swell. Pale moonlight sifted through the windows, high-lighting objects in the room, casting enormous shadows beyond. A faint snoring sound issued from the depths of an upholstered chair. Engstrom. Steam chuckled throatily in the radiator and the darkness was pleasant and warm. McBride reached for the bedlamp.

With the light came the brittle crackle of glass and something red hot seared McBride's side and went on to knock over the lamp. Black darkness swallowed the room. It seemed a long time before he heard the sound of the shot. Engstrom came out of the chair like a herd of elephants. "What was that?"

"Shut up!" McBride said. He lay there quietly, drawing long, careful breaths, trying to keep his heart from flopping out of his mouth. He was scared stiff. There were no more shots. He put his hand to the burning flesh coating his ribs and his fingers came away sticky. Presently he said, "Why, the dirty lice!"

"Who?" Engstrom asked.

"I don't think they left their cards," McBride said carefully. He got out of bed and approached the window. Moonlight silvered his bare feet. He looked out. Across the hollow square of the court the far wall was checkered with lighted windows. None of them was open. He looked at the neat round hole in the glass and drew an imaginary line from this to where he had lain. Following this line in the other direction he came to the conclusion that the shot had come from the roof of the other wing. He drew the blinds slowly, so that there would be no flicker of movement. He pulled the cord of the heavy drapes. He then went over and snapped the wall switch. Warm blood saturated the left sleeve of his pajamas where he held it against his side.

Engstrom looked at him stupidly. He was still holding McBride's gun.

"For Pete's sake, put that thing down!" McBride said sharply.

Engstrom said, "Hey, you're all bloody!" He looked sick.

"A mere scratch," McBride said, trying to be nonchalant. "It wasn't you that got shot, you know."

Engstrom pushed McBride down on the bed and went into the bathroom. After a while, using adhesive to stick a neat gauze pad in place, he surveyed McBride's torso critically. "What's all these other scars?"

"M'operations," McBride said sleepily.

"They don't look like operations to me."

McBride sat up. "Oh, you wanna argue, hunh?" He sulked. "All right, I'm a World War vet'ran."

"You're not old enough, you dope!"

"Well, can I help it?" McBride demanded.

Engstrom gave it up. "What you need is something to eat."

"That's a good idea," McBride said. He was suddenly and acutely conscious that he had missed lunch and if he didn't hurry he would miss dinner. "In fact, that's a swell idea. In fact, Engie, ol' pal, I'm dining with a lady. A lady *and* her husband."

He and Engstrom descended to the lobby half an hour later.

Engstrom said, "Aren't you going to report the shooting?"

McBride looked at him. "Do you think I should?"

"Certainly."

"Then I won't," McBride said. He stalked out to the cab. It had turned quite a lot colder since the rain, and the air was sharp and clear and bracing. It made McBride's lungs feel good.

Getting out of the cab in front of the Carmichael bungalow he said, "I'll be here for an hour or two, pal. I'll call you at the hotel." He went up the drive.

He was not conscious of going quietly; he had no thought other than dinner, and the possibility that by thus cultivating Carmichael he might be admitted to the inner circle. If there was an inner circle. Carmichael, he felt, was not quite sure of him yet. He turned off the drive onto a series of stepping stones which led to the front porch. Light from one of the front windows made a yellow path across the lawn, and without any idea of prying, McBride's glance followed the path to the window itself. He seemed destined at this house to be a Peeping Tom.

Mrs. Carmichael and a man who certainly was not Mr. Carmichael were having themselves a time. They stood almost directly beneath the ceiling chandelier and McBride's first thought was that there must be a piece of mistletoe tied to it. Then he remembered that it was a little early for Christmas. He knew the man was not Carmichael because Carmichael was even taller than McBride, and this man was short.

They broke finally, and McBride's heart almost stopped. The man was Mr. Erin Rourke. McBride thought, "Well, for the love of Mike, what is this?" He was a little dazed by the revelation that the voluble and rotund vice president of Acme Indemnity, and member of the board of the Underwriters' Alliance, should not only know Mrs. Carmichael, but obviously be on rather intimate terms with her. He wondered if Mr. Carmichael knew about it. And by the way, where *was* Mr. Carmichael?

The lady was laughingly removing a last trace of lipstick from the upturned visage of Erin Rourke. "The rat!" McBride muttered. He turned and ran back the way he had come. There was a tall hedge bordering the drive on one side; a clump of night-blooming jasmine on the left, where the drive met the sidewalk. The smell of it was heavy, cloyingly sweet in McBride's nostrils as he merged with its shadow, pretending that he too was a night-blooming jasmine. He was breathing a little hard.

PRESENTLY the front door opened and Mr. Erin Rourke came out. To some inquiry of the woman he said, "No, I think I'll walk." He picked his way along the stepping stones. The door closed. Small feet hurried down the drive. McBride took his gun out of his pocket, folded his fist over it, waiting. He waited till Rourke was exactly two feet beyond him before he stepped out and clouted the smaller man neatly behind the ear. Rourke didn't even gurgle. He just folded quietly to his knees, and McBride caught him, lifted him and carried him to the far side of the tall hedge. He didn't dare use a light, because there was a bungalow over here too. Rapidly, by sense of touch alone, he emptied Rourke's pockets of everything that was likely to hold a clue. Mindful that Rourke, and possibly the police, would worry about the motive for the attack, McBride even removed the loose change from Rourke's pants. He didn't leave him a nickel. Whistling through his teeth he walked rapidly away toward the blaze in the sky which was downtown Palos Verde.

On a corner four or five blocks away from his crime he found a market with a phone booth in it. He called the Carmichael residence. He decided that Erin Rourke must still be sleeping peacefully beside the hedge, or had taken his leave without disturbing Mrs. Carmichael. Her voice was quite composed. "Yes?"

McBride identified himself. "I wasn't sure whether I had promised definitely to come to dinner. Were you expecting me?"

"Yes, I was, Mr. McBride. That is, Mr. Carmichael phoned me to say he'd invited you. He'd forgotten that this was the maid's night off, but that wouldn't have made any difference. We intended to go out somewhere."

"Is Mr. Carmichael there now?"

She hesitated. "No, as a matter of fact, he isn't. He telephoned again to say that he had to go up to the dam. They're having trouble up there."

"What kind of trouble?" McBride said sharply.

She was vague about this. "The rain, I think. The river is flooding or something. Can't we have dinner somewhere—just you and I? Mr. Carmichael would—"

"All right," McBride said. He thought swiftly. "Tell you what. I'll send a cab out for you."

"That won't be necessary, Mr. McBride. I have my own car." She giggled a little. "But how will we know each other?"

"What kind of car do you drive?"

"A LaSalle coupé."

"Okay, I'll be outside the Grand National looking for you." He started to hang up, heard a bell ring at the other end, heard the woman's muffled scream. He depressed the receiver gently. Rourke had apparently returned to the house. McBride went out of the market and was lucky enough to catch a cab just discharging a fare. He rode the rest of the way downtown.

THERE was no sign of Engstrom outside the hotel. McBride supposed the guy had to eat the same as everybody else. He wished that he could eat. Going through the lobby he glowered at the crowd in the main dining room; the lesser, more vociferous crowd in the grill. Food smells gnawed at him. Music, he thought. Lights, laughter, food. For everybody but McBride. He wondered why as leisure-loving a guy as he should always be so busy. He went up in an elevator, examining the other passengers with a very personal interest. He was still mindful of the rifle shot from the roof. Nobody in the car looked malignant. No one else got out at his floor. He still wasn't taking any chances, though. He approached his door with extreme caution, stood far to one side and rattled the knob experimentally. Nothing happened. He inserted his key and flung the door inward. There wasn't any sudden fusillade of shots. From the darkness Engstrom's voice said, "Well, if you're coming in why don't you?"

McBride cursed. "How did you get in here?"

The ceiling lights went on. Engstrom walked into sight. He

had a gun. He grinned. "I used to be in the hardware business. I thought I told you."

McBride went in, slamming the door. "What'd you do, steal half the stock when they closed you up?" He looked at Engstrom's gun. "You got any more like that?"

"Sure."

"You're nothing but a crook," McBride said. He emptied his pockets of the loot he'd stripped from Erin Rourke. "Just a lousy crook, that's all."

"Youse hurt me, pal," Engstrom said cheerfully. He watched McBride sorting the stuff on the dresser top. "You seem to be doing pretty well, yourself. You kill the guy?"

McBride whirled. "What guy?"

"How should I know, pal? Maybe you didn't kill him, for all I know."

"Well, don't go accusing people then," McBride said. He returned to his inventory. There was a well-filled wallet, a card case, a couple of letters addressed to Mr. Erin Rourke. One of the letters was postmarked Palos Verde. It was from Mrs. Rourke, asking for money. The guy had told the truth about this, at least. The other letter was an old one, and, as far as McBride could see, unimportant. The keyfold looked interesting. There were three keys in particular. The stamped numbers indicated safety deposit boxes, though where the boxes were located was a deep dark mystery. McBride thought that probably he could find out. He was a little disappointed in the net result of his haul. In reality all he had was the information that Erin Rourke was the renter of three deposit boxes. While three seemed at least one too many for an honest man to possess, still it could be. Rourke was big business.

Rourke's visit to Palos Verde could easily be for the purpose he'd mentioned. All you had left, then, was the man's undeniable connection with Mrs. Carmichael. This didn't look so good. Rourke, as an official of the Underwriters' Alliance, should be concerned with Leeds & Leeds; not with the Five Companies.

Did his attraction for Mrs. Carmichael include Mr. Carmichael too? In other words, had Rourke met the wife through an earlier association with the husband? Had this association been a business one? Try as he would, McBride couldn't find a satisfactory motive for Erin Rourke to cross up his own company and his affiliates in the Alliance.

Sighing, he copied down the numbers on the three keys. This was a sort of automatic gesture. He expected nothing to come of it. In the act of bunching together Mr. Rourke's effects McBride was struck by remembrance of an earlier thought. Someone—someone here in Palos Verde—had murdered the hardware salesman, a man whose only crime lay in his sartorial resemblance to McBride. This implied a foreknowledge of McBride's arrival. Rourke could have telephoned or wired this information. So could Miss Ford. Or Sheila. Or Mr. Franz Charles, or the senior Leeds or any one of the dozen men who had been present when McBride was hired. McBride sighed again. Nothing there. Not even a good motive. Until he had actually uncovered something McBride was of no danger to anyone. He didn't think the guys behind this were the kind to get panicky at the mere thought of another detective.

All right, how about this last attack? That hadn't been meant to frighten; it had been meant to kill. Someone undoubtedly believed that McBride had found something. The way news travelled in this town—take Lou Queen's warning, for instance—it was possible that McBride's real reason for contacting Swiggart was no longer a secret. It could be assumed that Swiggart had talked. Hence the attempt to eliminate the man he might have talked to.

There was also the matter of Swiggart's money, allegedly stolen from police headquarters. If it had been stolen, and not for its intrinsic value, but because it was a link in the chain leading to the man or men behind Swiggart, then the thief had good reason to fear McBride. McBride had said he could identify the money. He looked at the section of picture mould behind which he had hidden the two bills he'd gotten from the

Mexican dancer, Juanita. He thought that perhaps he had better keep an eye on Juanita. Somebody might have wondered if Swiggart hadn't given her part of the money, just as McBride had wondered.

McBride got a blank Manila envelope from the desk, using a handkerchief to avoid leaving fingerprints. He put Rourke's personal property, with the exception of the money, in the envelope and sealed it. He then gave Engstrom a pencil. "Better print this," he said. He dictated: "Mr. Erin Rourke, Hotel Grand National."

Engstrom printed as directed. He was a swell printer. McBride nodded approvingly. "Fine." Engstrom, estimating the Rourke monies, leered. "Nice haul, pal." He smacked his lips. "Nice."

McBride was righteously indignant. "You think I'm a thief?"

"You're damned right I do," Engstrom said.

McBride looked at him. "You know, Engie, I think I'm going to like you. You're about the only guy in Palos Verde who isn't curious about my business. At that it's a relief to find somebody I can talk to—somebody with morals as low as mine."

Engstrom nodded sagely. "I could be a lot of help to you."

"Yeah," McBride sneered, "for forty bucks a day! You know what you are, Engie? You're a paid mercenary, that's what you are."

"Not yet I'm not," Engstrom said. "So far I ain't seen a dime of your money." He looked at the Manila envelope. "So now that you've implicated me, what do I do with this?"

McBride thought. "It better be delivered from somewhere outside the hotel. Find a kid that won't recognize you later."

Engstrom looked at his reflection in the mirror. "That ought to be easy. With my face in this condition even my own mother wouldn't recognize me."

"Dope!" McBride said. "This is serious. If the thing is traced back to you, and you're traced back to me—"

Engstrom shuddered. "Don't tell me, pal. I don't even want

to guess." He slit his throat with an index finger. "So you really killed the guy, hunh?"

"No!"

"Thanks, pal," Engstrom said. He went out.

CHAPTER XV

DEATH TO A DANCER

THE DESK AT the Grand National Hotel was always a busy place. With the town running wide open night and day, with salesmen, engineers, divorcees and tourists checking in and out at all hours there was scarcely a time when you didn't have to wait in line to get your chance at a clerk.

McBride, hurrying through the lobby to keep his date with Mrs. Carmichael, barely glanced at the knot of prospective guests. He was very surprised indeed when someone touched his arm and said, "Why, Rex McBride—how nice!"

The owner of the voice turned out to be Miss Ford. Beyond her was the very tall, very distinguished Mr. Franz Charles. The chairman of the Alliance of Pacific-Southwest Underwriters was not happy. His aquiline, aristocratic face was even bleaker than usual. His eyes speared McBride. "Well," he said. "Well."

McBride's gaze went from one to the other, linking them. "Quite a social season we're having." His tone was an insult.

Charles was annoyed. Miss Ford hastened to explain that this was not a social affair. "You're forgetting that I'm a secretary, aren't you?"

"Not necessarily," McBride said. "I've never possessed a secretary myself, but I understand they're very nice." He looked at Mr. Charles. "So this is strictly business?"

"It is," Charles said grimly. "I'm up here for a conference with Colin Leeds. His father has had a nervous breakdown."

McBride managed to make even his shrug an insult. "You don't have to explain your actions to me."

Charles colored. His retort was forestalled by the advent of Mr. Erin Rourke. Rourke's clothes looked as though he'd slept in them and he had a lump behind his ear the size of a golf ball. He was not glad to see Charles. "What are *you* doing here?"

"I might ask you the same thing," Charles said. "For myself this is purely business."

Rourke looked at Miss Ford. "Monkey business, I'll bet." He transferred his sharp eyes to McBride's inscrutable face, but apparently this told him nothing. He sighed. One small plump hand caressed the lump behind his ear. "I had a little accident," he said. He watched McBride's eyes.

McBride said carelessly, "Think nothing of it, pal. This town's full of accidents."

Franz Charles was irritated. "Too damned many if you ask me!"

McBride wondered if the flooding river could be construed as an accident. He said, "That's one thing you can't blame the Five Companies for."

Charles glared at him. "That reminds me, McBride, I hear you're working for Carmichael. That rather puts us on opposite sides of the fence, doesn't it?"

"Or the dam," McBride said. He put a question: "Any danger of the rain doing any real damage?"

Rourke's voice was heavily sarcastic. "Oh, no. No, indeed, Mr. McBride. The only thing the flood has done is carried away about eighty thousand dollars' worth of equipment which somebody mysteriously forgot about."

"Well, don't glare at me," McBride said. "I admit I did it." He put on his hat. "With my little hatchet," he added. He looked at Miss Ford. "Well, I mustn't keep you folks from your *business*." He went out.

Mrs. Carmichael's car was just drawing up to the curb. McBride thought she'd probably driven around the block three

*"We want you, McBride,"
said the chief from the
doorway, "for the murder
of the Mexican dancer."*

or four times after delivering Mr. Rourke. He went over. "Mrs. Carmichael?"

"Mr. McBride?" She was an ash blonde. She leaned toward him and the scent of Nuit d'Amour was like a blow between the eyes. "I'm sorry if I've kept you waiting."

"You haven't," he said, watching her. "I met an old friend of mine inside. A Mr. Erin Rourke."

Her face told him nothing. She was politely interested, no more. "Is he as romantic as his name sounds, Mr. McBride?"

"He's quite a guy with the ladies, all right." He turned and looked over his shoulder. Kay Ford and Erin Rourke were both watching him. Their expressions could have been stamped from the same mould. McBride wondered which would like to kill him most. He opened the car door hastily. "Mind walking a block or two, Mrs. Carmichael? I mean, there's no use taking the car. I thought we could drop in at the Natividad."

"All right," she agreed. She slid from the seat, exposing a

well-turned leg. She looked like a million. She was wearing a
three-quarter-length skunk. McBride still wasn't crazy about
blondes, but if he had liked blondes he would have been crazy
about Mrs. Carmichael. He wondered what she saw in her dour
husband. Or, for that matter, in the even less romantic Erin
Rourke. He gallantly offered her an arm and they walked the
block and a half to the Club Natividad. His spine tingled
because he knew that the thoughts, if not the eyes, of Rourke
and Miss Ford were on him. He didn't think they were nice
thoughts.

THEY went in by way of the casino. This was a big barn of a
room, carpeted but very gaudy with neon tubing and oils that
made up in significance what they lacked in art. Ceiling chan-
deliers of crystal were unable to cope with the layer upon layer
of smoke drifting up from the crowded layouts. Again McBride
marveled at the incongruity of pallid city men in white ties and
tails rubbing elbows with booted, none-too-clean muckers from
the dam. A woman who could have hailed from Boston's Back
Bay leaned over and kissed the bald spot on a grizzled hunky's
head. For luck, she said. The man with her didn't seem to mind.
He called the croupier a dirty name for shorting his stack of
chips.

McBride's hands began to sweat as he watched the stick man
at the nearest crap table. A hell of a note, he thought. I'm supposed to be a gambler and I haven't laid a dollar on the line
since I've been in town. He decided he'd have to remedy the
situation, but this would have to wait. He was hungry. He asked
Mrs. Carmichael if she was. He had to repeat the question
because she didn't hear him the first time. Her eyes were glued
to the wheel nearest her. Oh-oh, he thought, so the gal likes to
play games, hunh?

She looked at him vaguely. "Eat? Oh, of course. That's what
we came here for, isn't it?" She giggled a little. "I wish I could
leave the wheels alone. They're all crooked."

"Is that a fact!"

She said that it was. She said, "I dropped fifteen thou—fifteen *hundred* dollars here night before last." Her eyes slanted at his face to see whether he'd caught her slip. Apparently he hadn't. She looked relieved.

They went through an arch and up two steps to the supper room. Van himself, the very fat and allegedly very genial host of the Natividad, piloted them to a ringside table. The floor show was just going on. McBride watched Van seating other late diners. He wondered why Van had refused to surrender his hat to the plane hostess the first time McBride had seen him. He wondered why, if the gray man, Train, controlled the town and probably Van too, they hadn't exchanged a word during that whole first trip. Not even riding the bus with McBride.

Mrs. Carmichael said, "You're not having a very good time, are you?"

He'd practically forgotten her for a moment. He said, "I'm sorry." His voice became a caress. "Really, I hadn't meant to neglect you, Mrs. Carmichael. I was just thinking that your husband must make a nice thing out of the Five Companies to let you drop fifteen hundred of an evening."

Her eyes were suddenly haunted. She leaned across the table toward him. "Do me a favor?"

She crumpled her napkin, avoiding his eyes. "I can be very nice to people I like, Mr. McBride."

Remembering Erin Rourke, he thought this was probably a fact. His voice warmed a trifle. "What do I do to make you like me?"

"Forget the money I mentioned."

He patted her hand. "I'll even do better than that. I'll lend you the dough."

"You will?"

He wished she wasn't a blonde. He waved violently for his waiter. "A couple of martinis, very dry. And rush those steaks, will you?"

The waiter said he would do this. He went away. McBride,

half his mind on the floor show, was startled when it ended abruptly without the advertised dance routines of Juanita. He asked the waiter about this when he brought the martinis.

The man said, "I don't know, sir. I could ask Mr. Van."

"Never mind," McBride said. He rose as the orchestra broke into a rhumba. "Dance?"

She came into his arms easily, gracefully, and they moved out onto the floor. Hers was the first corseted waist he'd had under his hand for years. Nuit d'Amour almost strangled him. He was glad when the dance ended. Returning to the table he swallowed his martini in one gulp.

With the steaks came the mountainous Mr. Van. Rolls of fat obscured his collar and as he bent his large head to survey McBride his black tie seemed fastened to the lower of his three chins, like a comedy beard. "You are asking about Juanita. Why?"

"What do you mean—why? Why shouldn't I ask about her? You advertise her, don't you? She's included in the price of steaks, isn't she?" McBride rather overdid the irate customer.

Van pinched his lower lip between a fat thumb and forefinger. "I beg your pardon, sir." His voice was as smooth and unpleasant as castor oil. "We've been rather worried about her ourselves. She has never been this late before."

"So what do I do—cry?"

"You do nothing, Mr. McBride, absolutely nothing." Van moved ponderously away. McBride had the sense of missing something significant but for a full minute he didn't get it. Then he did and it was like a cold shower. The fat man had called him by name.

MRS. CARMICHAEL watched his vicious attack on the steak. "I don't like him either," she said. "Funny how you don't like people you owe."

"Never a truer word was spoke," McBride said. He buttered a hot roll, considering her. She didn't look dumb. She looked, in fact, like a very smart number—for a blonde. Maybe, he thought, she's trading me all this information on the strength of the fifteen C's I promised her. It was interesting to know that she owed Van dough; money her husband wasn't supposed to hear about. He wondered how much she really owed the fat guy, and what Van hoped to get in lieu of money. He wondered if Van knew that Swiggart had been running around with the Mexican girl Juanita. He decided that he disliked Mr. Van as much as he feared Mr. Train, though with no more reason. He finished his steak. He said, "You know, it's a funny thing, babe, but I still don't know what your husband's official title is."

She looked at him. "He's vice president in charge of operations."

He whistled. "Big shot, hunh?" After a while he said in a puzzled voice, "But there aren't any operations here. Not Five Companies operations."

"No?"

He had a momentary flash of insight. All this talk of the money she owed Van, and the pretense of making him a conspirator against her husband could be part of a well-laid plan. In other words she could be testing his loyalty to Carmichael. Even the absence of Carmichael could be accounted for in this way. Against this theory you had her clandestine affair with Erin Rourke and the undeniable fever in her eyes as she watched the roulette wheel. Just the same, he decided to tighten up.

As though sensing this new suspicion on his part and afraid she'd lost him, Mrs. Carmichael said hurriedly, almost breathlessly, "You used to work for the Underwriters' Alliance, didn't you?"

"Unh-hunh."

"But you aren't any more?"

He elaborately concealed a yawn. "Baby, a private dick is just like any other dick. Remove the hokum and you'll find that the regular cops work for money just like the rest of us. The only thing is, the average shamus is smart enough to work for the highest bidder. As long as your husband is the highest bidder I'm working for him."

She dropped her eyes. "I've heard stories of men who played both ends against the middle."

"But not for long, babe. If you'd followed those stories to their logical conclusion you'd find that those same guys are either broke or dead. It happens I'm neither."

She sighed. "But what about poor little me? If you're loyal to my husband how do I know you won't tell him about—about us?"

He grinned at her. "It has been said that you mustn't mix business with pleasure." He stood up. "And this has been a pleasure, hasn't it?"

She rose too, leaning toward him. "The first of many, I hope."

"Me too," he said. He paid their check, waited while she got her things. They walked back to her car in front of the Grand National. He helped her in. "Look, about that dough I promised you—"

Her eyes, wide with sudden fright, were looking past him. McBride turned casually. Mr. Carmichael, the lady's husband, was almost at his elbow. "Hello, McBride. Have a nice time?"

"Swell," McBride said. "Sorry you missed it." He watched Carmichael. "I was just telling your wife I was sorry she had to pay the check. I came away without my wallet. I'll send it around in the morning."

"Forget it." Carmichael leaned forward a little to study his wife's face. McBride wished she didn't look so scared. He still couldn't make up his mind whether she was two-timing him or her husband. The only thing he was sure of was that he had seen her kissing Erin Rourke in anything but a platonic manner. Come to think of it, she had pretended Rourke was an utter stranger. Well, the hell with that now. McBride was in something of a hurry to get away.

He said, "If you'd care to wait I could get the money now."

"Forget it," Carmichael said again. His voice was harsh, with an edge to it. He jammed his long length into the seat beside his wife. "Get going, Gwen." They rolled out into the stream of traffic.

"SO HER name is Gwendolyn," McBride thought. Still pondering this he moved down the cab rank till he spotted Engstrom. "Hello, pal."

Engstrom was morose. "It's started already," he said.

"What has?"

"Blackmail," Engstrom said. After a while he said. "That kid!"

"What kid?"

"The one I give that envelope to. Naturally when I tell him not to mention me he smells something. He's been back twice."

McBride took a breath. "How much he take you for?"

"It ain't the money," Engstrom said gloomily. "It's the principle of the thing."

McBride scowled. "How much?"

Engstrom avoided his eyes. "A quarter."

McBride shook with sudden mirth. "Imagine that!" He got into the cab. "A whole quarter?"

Engstrom sulked. "Like I told you, it's the principle—"

"Yeah," McBride jeered, "you probably gave the kid a nickel in the first place. Serves you right for being Scotch."

"I'm not Scotch," Engstrom said heatedly. "I'm Norwegian."

"Bragging, hunh?" McBride unfolded one of the jump seats, put his feet on it. "Okay, Viking, heave ho for that court you took me to this morning." He dozed comfortably, not even thinking, till the cab drew up in front of the double row of bungalows.

There were lights on in most of them. It was only about nine o'clock. A couple came out of the first unit on the right, looked at McBride as he came up the walk. He pulled his hat down over his eyes, waiting till they had turned into the street. The third unit on the left was dark. It had the indefinable air of having been dark all evening. A late edition of the *Argus* lay on the small stoop.

McBride rang the bell. After a while he rang again. Getting no answer he tried the knob. The door was locked. Across the court a radio blared noisily. A man came out of one of the rear units and passed McBride furtively, on his way to the street. McBride had a sudden overwhelming urge to see what lay behind that locked door. He stepped down off the stoop, put a steady even pressure on the French windows about where he thought the catch ought to be. There was the brittle sound of snapping metal, scarcely discernible above the radio music, and something fell to the floor inside. McBride slid over the sill into a bedroom.

He didn't move for a full moment, just stood there quietly in the dark, listening. There was no sound other than a dripping water tap somewhere close at hand, probably in the bath. He closed the windows, muting the blatant radio across the way, and listened some more. Stale incense offended his nostrils. The air in the place was stifling. Presently, assured that he was alone, he drew the curtains over the windows and struck a match. The bed had not been slept in. There were clothes scattered about, and in the closet he found more clothes and a small pile of luggage. Juanita, then, had not left town. He snapped on the lights and went through into the living room. The windows here were already covered. He pulled the chain of a floor lamp and soft rose light flooded the divan.

Juanita lay among the batik cushions. She had been dead for quite a while, McBride thought. Her black eyes were wide, starey, a little frightened. From between her small breasts protruded the haft of the knife she herself had used that morning. McBride went over and touched her. Her flesh was cold. He gagged a little as he saw that he had gotten a smear of blood on his fingers. He bent and wiped it off on the rug. Then, very low, he said, "I'm sorry, kid." His face was so stiff it hurt.

CHAPTER XVI

THE BACK ROOM

THE HONKY-TONK ON B Street was almost deserted. A couple of late customers drank quietly at the bar, but the B-girls were leaving them strictly alone. The girl McBride had bribed was not in sight. He asked a bartender if he could see Lou Queen and the guy hauled a phone out from under the bar and spoke into it. He replaced the phone. "Stick around for a while. I'll let you know when."

McBride went over to a table where three of the girls were sitting. "Hello, kids." There was a half-hearted chorus of hellos in reply, but none of the three bothered to even ask him to buy a drink. He got the impression that they were all scared to death. He tried dropping nickels in the player piano to sort of liven the atmosphere, but his heart wasn't in it. He remembered that the last guy he had seen doing this was now dead.

He swung around to face the nearest girl. "What's the idea? Am I poison or something?"

She shrugged. "You should see Maggie's eye."

Maggie, he guessed, was the girl he'd asked about Swiggart. "Lou?" he said. All he got for his pains was an insolent stare. He said, "You tell Maggie I'm sorry about that." He got out a twenty, ostentatiously laid it on the piano. "For Maggie's eye." He had to put a quarter in the player because he didn't have any more nickels. He listened to a re-hash of *St. Louis Blues*.

After a while the bartender came over and told him that Lou Queen would see him now. He followed the guy up the carpeted stairs to a room that looked as though a Hollywood art director had had a hand in decorating it. It was done in whites and off-whites, picked out here and there with silver. Even the inch-deep carpet was white. McBride felt as though he were wading across to the woman on the chaise longue.

She was in green, giving the effect of an emerald set in platinum. Her white hair was done high on her head and diamond pendants dripped light from her ear lobes. Her beautiful eyes were the exact shade of her gown.

He drew his breath in sharply. "Marvelous!"

"Sit down, McBride."

He sat, watching her. She was the most beautiful thing he had ever seen, not even excepting Kay Ford. Strangely, though, he had no desire to touch her. He was content merely to look at her, let her seep into his senses, like a drug.

She said, "Things getting pretty warm for you, McBride?"

"How do you mean?"

She moved her bare shoulders, settling herself more comfortably among the cushions. When she spoke it was half to herself, as though she didn't care whether he were listening or not. Her voice was low and rich, and, despite the idiom of the street, curiously compelling. Somehow it reminded McBride of another voice, Train's. He shivered a little. She said, "In my racket you get so you think of men as just pocketbooks, but once in a blue moon you meet a guy you could really like. You like the way they work, even though you don't always know what they're trying to do. You got anything to tell me, McBride?"

The logs in the white fireplace burned slowly, evenly, without crackling. It was very quiet in the room. McBride didn't look at her as he answered: "No."

"You're not very smart, McBride."

"You're telling me!"

She turned lazily on one hip, reaching for a cigarette. "Swiggart wasn't very smart either, was he?"

McBride thrust his chair back angrily. "Damn it, Lou, I didn't come here to talk business!"

"The hell you didn't," she said calmly. "Why do you suppose I had you brought up here instead of to the office? Why do you think I'm dolled up fit to kill?"

He shrugged. "I don't know."

"Then I'll tell you, McBride. I wanted to check something I was pretty sure of before. You know you haven't even kissed me?"

He grinned. "That can be remedied, Lou." He bent over her. "I couldn't bear to muss you up."

She pushed him away. "Nuts." She swung her long legs off the chaise, sitting up. "Look, boy, you're not interested in me any more than you would be in a beautiful picture. You're working. You were working the first time you came here."

"You shouldn't have blacked Maggie's eye," he said.

"I should have kicked her out of here. In this racket the girls don't discuss one customer with another." She got up, kicking the train of her gown out of her way. "Who are you working for?"

"Carmichael."

"You're a liar."

"All right," he shrugged, "ask him."

SHE MOVED slowly over to the mantel. Yellow and blue flames outlined her perfect form through the green gown. "Lord," he said huskily, "you're beautiful!"

"Thanks, pal." Idly she picked up an ivory-framed miniature. There were two likenesses in it. One was of herself, apparently taken years before. The other was—McBride caught his breath. Time had changed him, but there was no doubt that it was the gray man, Train, who looked out of the double frame at McBride. He removed his eyes with difficulty. The woman put the miniature back on the mantel. "You kill Swiggart, McBride?"

"No."

"How about the girl Juanita?"

Startled, he turned furious eyes on her. "So you know about that too!"

"I hear things," she admitted calmly.

He took a step toward her. "Then tell me who did it!"

"I don't know, McBride."

"You're lying!" he said passionately. His fingers bit into her bare shoulders. "You're lying and I'm not going to stand for it!"

She didn't move. "You're hurting me, McBride."

His hands dropped away and he flushed dully as he saw the marks his fingers had left on her white flesh. "I'm sorry, Lou."

"Sure."

She's trying to tell me something, he thought. She's got some kind of an object in letting me see that picture of her and Train. His mind went back to that first plane trip out from Los Angeles. The three of them—Van, Lou Queen and St. George Train could have been total strangers. Not one of them had acknowledged by word or look that he knew the others. Yet manifestly this was impossible. Train was supposed to run Palos Verde. Obviously he couldn't run it without knowing the others. There was something going on under the surface here; something that might or might not be connected with the sabotage at the dam. McBride wished he was more sensitive, more receptive to impressions.

He took a turn up and down the room. "I've the feeling that you're trying to use me somehow. What is it you want?"

Her laugh was cynically amused. "What have you got to give a woman like me?" She made an impatient gesture as he frowned. "Look, McBride, come clean with me. Who are you working for?"

His face was wooden. "I told you."

"And you lied. A guy like you doesn't play stooge for a mug like Carmichael. You're no penny-ante bodyguard."

"Read the papers," he said. "A private dick will do anything."

"Maybe some private dicks." Her green eyes fastened on him eagerly. "Look, if I tell you how I knew about the girl Juanita will that prove I'm on the level?"

"You don't have to tell me. I think you're on the level anyway."

She opened her mouth to say something, closed it abruptly as a buzzer sounded somewhere in the room.

ALMOST immediately the hall door was flung inward and Chief Beale stood there, short legs spread, a look of surprised satisfaction on his ruddy face. He had a gun in his hand. Behind him towered his brother Harry.

Lou Queen said, "Hello, heel."

The chief was pained. "Now, Lou—" His ball-bearing eyes rolled over to McBride. "We want you, pal."

"For what?"

"For the murder of Juanita Mendota."

McBride's eyes didn't even flicker. "I don't believe I know the lady."

Harry Beale laughed boomingly, as if this were a great joke. "You don't have to know 'em to kill 'em, pal." He squeezed past his brother and McBride saw that he too had a gun. "But we can talk over the petty details down at Headquarters. No use bothering the lady." He gestured with the gun. "Coming quietly, McBride?"

McBride shrugged. "Why not?"

Lou Queen said, "Now wait a minute, when did all this happen?"

Chief Beale coughed delicately. "Doc says a little after seven this evening, Lou. Why?"

She laughed. "A fine bunch of cops you are! At seven tonight McBride was with me. He's been with me ever since."

"We heard different," Beale said mildly. "In fact he was seen having dinner with another—uh—lady around eight or a little after. You keep your nose clean, Lou."

McBride looked at her. "Thanks for trying, pal. There's nothing to it, anyway. They haven't got a thing."

"That's the spirit," Harry Beale nodded. "Give me a guy that stands on his own legs; a guy that don't go around hiding behind women's skirts."

The chief sounded apologetic as hell. "I'm sorry we had to bust in on you like this, Lou. You know how it is—"

She ignored him. "Let me know how you come out, Rex."

"Sure." He walked to the door. "Come on, you guys, let's get it over with. I'm in a hurry." The Beales followed him down the stairs. A third dick was holding a gun on the big room below. He nodded sleepily at McBride, put his gun away. McBride shrugged into his overcoat. Someone had thoughtfully removed his gun from the right-hand pocket. The four went out and climbed in the chief's car and rode downtown. No one said anything more until they were closeted in the chief's office. Then Harry Beale pushed a chair forward. "Sit down, McBride."

"I don't want to sit down."

"I said to sit down."

McBride looked behind him and the sleepy-looking dick was hefting a sap. McBride sat down. Chief Beale moved the open newspaper on his desk, exposing a knife. The knife still had plenty of blood on it. "Ever see this before, McBride?"

"No."

Harry Beale chuckled throatily. "Maybe it was dark when he used it. It just sort of jumped into his hand without him seeing it."

His brother was only mildly annoyed. His eyes swiveled from Harry to McBride. "You remember when you first hit town we took a gun away from you?" Not waiting for McBride's answer he went on: "We had that little rod around for a while. Just in case we might need 'em later we made a record of your prints on it." He paused, savoring his next words. "Funny thing, Mr. McBride, we found the same set of prints on the haft of this little sticker."

McBride remembered then. He had handled the knife when he'd taken it away from Juanita. Whoever had used the thing afterward could conceivably have worn gloves, blurring McBride's prints perhaps, but not destroying them. He sat perfectly still.

"That's how we knew you did it," Chief Beale concluded.

McBride said nothing. There seemed nothing to say. If the girl Juanita had died at approximately seven o'clock then McBride was in no position to offer an alibi. At that time he had been busy spying on Erin Rourke and Mrs. Carmichael, later slugging Rourke and then walking for a number of blocks. Not that an alibi would be of much avail against the damning evidence of the prints.

Chief Beale got up and came around the desk. "All we got to do now is find out *why* you did it."

"I didn't do it," McBride said. He figured Harry as the dangerous one and was consequently watching Harry instead of the chief. This was his mistake. The chief took a sap out of his hip pocket and clouted McBride between the eyes. McBride and the chair went over backward, making quite a crash. The sleepy-looking dick stood with his back to the door. McBride got up, swaying.

The chief hit him again, this time on the neck. McBride's head snapped sideways and the room whirled dizzily. He thought his neck was broken. "I told you I hated you," the chief said. His voice sounded a million miles away.

McBride put his hands to his head, twisting it back and forth. It felt like a balloon but the room suddenly steadied. The chief's congested face came into direct focus and McBride swung at it. A length of rubber garden hose came out of nowhere and belted him in the teeth. He fell down. Somebody kicked him in the ribs, probably Harry. He lay quietly, not conscious of anything more for a while. When he did wake up he was once more in the chair.

"WHY, McBRIDE?" Chief Beale sounded very patient indeed. "Just tell us why and we'll let up on you."

Blood was salty on McBride's lips and darting little slivers of light, millions of them, slanted in front of his eyes. "Give me a drink," he said thickly.

"No."

He licked at the blood, felt blindly in his pockets for a handkerchief. He couldn't see a thing. He wondered if he'd ever see anything again. His lips were swollen from the blow on the mouth. He ran a fuzzy tongue over his teeth. As far as he could tell they were all intact, but talking was difficult at best. Thinking was even worse. He remembered foggily that his fight with Swiggart was supposed to have been over the girl. This and his prints on the murder weapon would be enough to hang him anywhere. He considered telling the truth, couldn't see that this would help him much. He tried it anyway. "I saw the girl this morning. She was sore about something and came at me with the knife. I took it away from her." Suddenly, the rain of light-darts stopped blinding him and he could see. "That's how my prints got on the knife."

Harry Beale came around from behind the chair. Harry now had a length of hose too. He hit McBride in the throat with it. "Tell the truth, you louse!"

McBride couldn't tell the truth. He couldn't even talk. He thought that probably his Adam's apple had been driven clear through to the back of his neck. He put up his hands weakly to ward off the next blow, but it didn't do any good. After a while he passed out.

CHAPTER XVII

A GUN UP HIS SLEEVE

ALCOHOL STUNG HIS bruised lips, sharply though not unpleasantly. It had the clean feel of antiseptic on a wound. Presently, when his sensory nerves were stimulated enough, he identified the fluid in his mouth as whisky and the hard object against his teeth as the neck of a bottle. He allowed some of the whisky to pass his tonsils. Pure agony followed this experiment. Apparently someone had sandpapered the inside of his throat. Choking, he sat up, and his eyes came open, mechanically, like those of a sleeping doll. Immediately he was sorry for this, because it was the gray man, Train, who was holding the bottle. McBride closed his eyes again, hoping it was just a figment of his imagination.

Train said, "Come on, McBride, snap out of it." The tone of his voice was as sweet, as compelling as an organ's alto. It reminded McBride of another voice with almost the same quality and this in turn took him through his arrest and the subsequent shellacking. He was wide awake when he opened his eyes for the second time. He ran his tongue around the inside of his lips. He could actually feel the imprint of his own teeth. Train said, "Ah, that's better!" He had the air of a healer of mankind.

Water drooled down out of McBride's hair into his eyes. He suspected that someone had emptied a bucket over him. He wiped his face on a coat sleeve. "Hello, Train."

Train made sympathetic noises.

McBride looked cautiously around. There was no one in the

room beside Train and himself. It was a strange room; that is, one that he had never been in before, though it had the indefinable air of a back room at any police headquarters in the world. A dingy yellow globe in the ceiling cast feeble light over bare whitewashed walls, a scarred oak table, two chairs and the sagging leather couch on which McBride sat. There were no windows in the room. McBride removed his eyes from the room's one door and looked at the bottle. He put out an unsteady hand. "Mind?"

"Not at all," Train said. He relinquished the bottle.

McBride drank greedily. The liquor bit into him like a slug in the stomach and he gagged a little, but did not throw up. Presently he set the bottle on the table and found a handkerchief and wiped at his mouth. There was not much blood left. He got up, trying his legs. They were a trifle weak. He sat down again. "Well, I guess I can take another round."

"You don't have to, McBride. You're out on bail."

"A murder rap isn't bailable," McBride said. "If I'm admitted to bail then I'm not guilty."

Train smiled. "You're probably guilty, my friend, and the rap still holds. It so happens, however, that I have some slight influence in Palos Verde and I've persuaded a magistrate friend of mine to make an exception in your case. We can walk out of here any time you're ready."

McBride found a soggy cigarette in one of his pockets, lit it, dragged smoke deep into his lungs. "That's nice of you, pal, but I think I'll stay here if you don't mind."

"And take another shellacking from the Beales?"

McBride thought about this for a while. He couldn't make up his mind which he feared most—another working over like the one he'd just gone through or the prospect of even worse at the hands of St. George Train. Finally he said just one word: "Why?"

"Why am I doing this for you?" Train shrugged well-tailored shoulders. "Really, I'm risking very little in posting bail for you,

McBride. You are too well-known to get very far in case you considered jumping your bond."

"All right, you're risking very little. I'm still asking—why spring me at all?"

Train smiled. "Perhaps I'm just curious about you, McBride. I'm always a bit curious about newcomers to my town—especially those who create as much excitement as you have. You amaze me, my boy, really you do."

"I even amaze myself sometimes," McBride admitted.

"Then it's a deal?"

"No," McBride said comfortably. "I like it here."

Train laughed musically. "Afraid of me, McBride?"

McBride stood up. He was afraid, but he wasn't going to admit it to this guy. "Let's go," he said. They went through the door and down the hall to the lobby. The desk sergeant saluted Train as if he were the Tsar of all the Russias. He handed McBride his hat and coat. "Better put 'em on," he advised. "You're all wet."

"I must be," McBride said, "when even a cop notices it." He looked at the closed door of Chief Beale's office, contemplated kicking it in, discarded the idea as being unfeasible at the moment and permitted Mr. Train to escort him out to the street. Engstrom's cab was at the curb. Engstrom pretended he didn't know McBride from Adam's off ox. He looked at Train. "Cab, sir?"

"No," Train said. He sounded a little absent. "No, thanks." He took McBride's arm. "Mind walking as far as your hotel?"

McBride said he didn't mind in the least. He was gratified that he was being taken to a place as public as the Grand National. He had no illusions about the spot he was in, though. Train, or anybody else, could shoot him down with impunity. His killer, indeed, would more than likely be considered a public benefactor, saving Palos Verde County the expense of a trial. They started walking.

IN THE second block McBride chanced to look in a shop window. This window formed part of a V entryway, angling enough to mirror the sidewalk behind them. There was a slender man, very natty in derby and dark Chesterfield, who seemed to be matching his pace to that of McBride and Train. His right hand was bulky in the side pocket of the Chesterfield.

McBride jerked his chin over his shoulder. "Yours?"

"Of course," Train said.

"Nice."

"Comfortable," Train said.

They walked on. In the lobby of the Grand National they waited for the man in the derby and Chesterfield to come through the doors. He had the unmistakable air of a gunsel. His thin dark eyebrows looked as though they had been plucked to harmonize with the hairline mustache on his upper lip. His eyes never seemed to settle directly on anything.

McBride said irritably, "Now what?"

Train appeared surprised. "Wouldn't you like to change clothes?"

Something about this struck McBride as very funny. He laughed. "My shroud?"

"A corpse should always be neat," Train agreed.

McBride caught a glimpse of himself in one of the big pier glasses. He looked disreputable. He was surprised they didn't throw him out. Just as he thought of this he saw the house dick bearing down on him from the elevators.

The guy puffed up. He was patently out of patience with McBride. "There's a bullet hole in one of your windows," he said accusingly.

"No!"

"And blood on your pajamas!"

"Is that a fact?" McBride seemed to be looking at the house dick but in reality he was studying Train. Train's face told him nothing. He said, "How did you find out about all this?"

"The valet. He went in after your clothes."

"Well, I'll tell you about it," McBride said. "My theory is that somebody was shooting ducks and—"

The house man snorted indignantly. "What was he in, a plane?"

"How should I know?"

"See here, Mr. McBride, I'll have to report this to the police."

"Good idea," McBride nodded. "I intended to do it myself, only I've been pretty busy."

The dick's eyes mirrored a suspicion that McBride was slightly on the wacky side. "You'll have to pay for the window."

"I will like hell!" McBride was outraged. "It wasn't me that busted it."

Train's laugh was softly musical. "Go away, Brody. Go peddle your papers somewhere else."

Brody said, "Yes, *sir!*" He went heavily away.

McBride looked at Train admiringly. "I guess you were right when you called this your town. Even the house dicks jump through hoops for you." He watched a small crowd come out of the bar. Kay Ford and Mr. Franz Charles passed within a yard of him. Neither paid him the slightest attention. He sighed. He faced Mr. Train resolutely. "How much was my bail set at?"

"Five grand."

"I don't like to be under obligations," McBride said. He crossed to the desk, asked a clerk for the envelope he had left in the safe. In a mirror he saw Train's gunsel turn slightly, so that the bulge in the Chesterfield's right-hand pocket pointed at the desk. Train appeared quietly at his elbow. He watched McBride count out five grand from the sheaf of bills. The two top bills, hundreds. McBride put carefully back in the envelope, substituting others. He did this ostentatiously. He gave the envelope back to the clerk. "Take good care of that, pal."

Train said, "See here, McBride, this isn't necessary."

McBride pressed the money on him. "I'm a funny guy, Train.

I just can't bear to owe a guy I'm liable to bust in the nose most any minute."

"I can see your point," Train said gravely. He put the bills away in his wallet. They crossed the lobby and entered an elevator. The gunsel had to hurry a little to make the same car. Neither Train nor McBride looked at him, not even when he followed them out and down to McBride's room. He stayed out in the hall, looking rather lonely, McBride thought. Train removed his hat and leaned against the only other possible exit, the communicating door to the next room. McBride was undecided whether the gray man carried a gun. He could see no evidence of it. He began shedding his clothes. "Is this to be a permanent arrangement?"

"It depends on you, my friend."

"Oh?" McBride was thinking furiously. Reversing the usual query he asked himself, "What have I got that he ain't got?" He thought about throwing a shoe at Mr. St. George Train, but there was always the hood outside. He wished the brothers Beale wouldn't keep on taking his gun away all the time.

TRAIN carefully clipped the end of a thin, dappled cigar. He was very deliberate about lighting it. "I understand you've been making inquiries about me."

"Who told you that?"

"A friend in Los Angeles. Your source is a clumsy oaf, even for a stockbroker."

"I didn't think so much of him either," McBride said. He was examining his face in the dresser mirror. It was swelled a little in spots but the skin was unbroken. He was grateful to the manufacturers of rubber hose. He said ruefully, "Well, I suppose you want to know why I was interested?"

"That's the general idea."

McBride turned. The adhesive on the pad under his arm had come loose and his undershirt was stained with fresh blood. He said, "I'm just one of the masses, I guess. Success always interests me. So I says to this guy—"

"Cut it," Train said. He blew a casual smoke ring. "Let's quit clowning around, McBride. You ought to know by this time that I can make or break you in Palos Verde. Also, you can't get out. Every road is watched and there are cops at the airport and at the station. One wrong move and you'll be shot down."

"Like a dog?" McBride suggested. "I've always wondered what it would be like to be shot down like a dog. I've been shot down plenty of other ways, but never—"

"I'm not fooling, McBride."

McBride sighed. "I didn't think you were." He paused in the business of laying out the fresh clothes returned by the valet service. "All right, you're not fooling. You want to know why I looked up your recent transactions in Leeds & Leeds Construction. So I want to know something too. I want to know why you had me sprung. And if that cheap gunsel of yours is going to smoke me why the hell don't he get it over with?"

Train waved his cigar. "There's no hurry. About my motive for springing you—well, let's say I'm just curious about how far you've gone with your investigation. What have you got, McBride?"

McBride cursed. "You're as bad as everybody else!" He stabbed a finger at Train's chest. "Look, I came up here for the Underwriters' Alliance. I admit it. But I didn't like the set-up, so I quit. I am now employed as a bodyguard for a guy named Carmichael and trying to get a little leisure to do some serious gambling. Is this helping you any?"

"And your inquiry about me?"

"That was before I quit."

Train studied the ash on his cigar. "I see." He put his uncomfortably direct stare on McBride's face. "You tell anybody about your discoveries?"

"Why should I?"

"You are a smart man, Mr. McBride. You are, in fact, an intelligent man. As a little tip I would suggest that you look up the date on which I made my first short sale." He put on his hat, moved toward the door. "Good night, Mr. McBride."

McBride said, "Well, shut my mouth!" He said, "Hey, wait! What is this, anyway?"

Train had a hand on the knob. "Really, McBride, I don't mind your antics in the least. You are, in fact, much more valuable to me on the loose than you would be in jail. Ergo, you are free." After a moment he added, "Up to a certain point, of course."

"Oh, of course!"

Without the slightest warning the door hurled inward and Mr. Train, being in front of the door, was hurled with it. He sprawled at McBride's feet. Engstrom, a rather wild-eyed Engstrom, stood in the opening brandishing a gun. "So!" he said.

McBride looked at him. "The Vikings to the rescue. You are very rude, Engie, coming in like that." He stooped, aiding Train to his feet. "Mr. Train was just going, Engie."

Train lifted an inquiring eyebrow at the empty hall. Engstrom sniffed. "Oh, that guy? He was a pushover." He made a chopping motion with the gun. "Just like that."

"I see," Mr. Train said. He recovered his hat. "Well, good night, Mr. McBride." He went out. Engstrom looked at the closed door, looked down at the gun in his fist. "I must be good, hunh?"

"No doubt of it," McBride said. He discovered that he had been holding his breath for at least a couple of hours. He let it out slowly, gratefully. "Dead people are good too, Engie. Remember that, will you? Train could have shot you full of holes while you stood there waving that cannon."

Engstrom was incredulous. "He never even had a gun!"

"That's what I thought too, pal. It seems I was wrong. He carries it in his sleeve."

CHAPTER XVIII

LINES TO L.A.

McBRIDE SAT ON the edge of the bed, a small table pulled up between his knees. He was fully dressed now and, except for a slight puffiness about his mouth and eyes, looked pretty good. On the table were a telephone, a scribbled sheet of paper and a .45 automatic. The gun was Engstrom's.

McBride lifted the phone. "Hi, babe."

"Why, *Mister* McBride!"

"You like those flowers I sent you?"

The operator said she certainly had. She said, "I like fur coats, too."

"Chiseler. Look, toots, I need a couple of clear lines into Los Angeles and a lot of privacy. You'll have to fake the charges to some other room or to the cash account."

"Do I get the fur coat?"

"Well, I don't know," McBride said cautiously. "What kind of fur?"

"How about skunk? Skunks are very inexpensive."

"Not the kind I know," McBride said. He added hastily, "No offense, babe. I didn't mean you."

"Oh." There was a brief pause before her voice came, very confidential and a little awed: "Mr. McBride, are you really a murderer?"

He sucked in his breath. So it was all over town, hunh? "Sure, babe, I love 'em and leave 'em—dead. Would you like to wear your fur coat to the funeral?"

"What funeral?"

"Yours."

"Mr. McBride, you're kidding!"

"You'll find out," he prophesied. "Here's the first number." He gave it to her and cradled the phone, waiting. He jacked the automatic open to be sure there was a cartridge in the chamber. There was. He watched the door. After a while the phone buzzed. "Los Angeles Police Department."

"Lieutenant Escobar," McBride said. Presently he said, "Escobar? Rex McBride. Look, how's about a favor?"

"Unh-unh, I'm broke."

"A fine cop!" McBride sneered. "Not only honest but bragging about it." He waited till the obscenities ceased. "All right, you're not honest then. So here's something that may or may not mean a promotion for you. If it does I'll drop the case in your lap." He read from the sheet of paper. "Those are safety deposit boxes. No, I don't know where, or whose name they're under. All I can do is tell you what the guy looks like." He described Erin Rourke, adding that Mr. Rourke was a vice president of Acme Indemnity. "I'd like to know what's in those boxes without the guy knowing I'm interested."

Escobar grumbled. "Even if I find 'em I'll have to get a court order. What's this guy done?"

"I think he killed his grandmother," McBride said. "You may find her in one of the boxes for all I know." He turned serious. "Look, fella, I'm in kind of a spot up here. You may not be able to reach me by phone in the morning, and anyway, incoming calls are liable to be watched."

"So what do I do?"

McBride thought. "Tell you what," he said presently. "If you find anything that looks screwy you call Sheila Mason, either at her home or at the office of Leeds & Leeds. I'm going to call her about something else and I'll tell her."

"Okay, heel." The phone clicked.

The operator downstairs broke in. "Oh, Mr. McBride, is that nice Mr. Rourke a murderer too?"

McBride gnashed his teeth. "Listen," he grated, "I asked for a clear line. You keep on listening in and it gives no skunk coats. It gives a kick in the teeth."

"Yes, Mr. McBride. What number are you calling, please?"

He gave her Sheila's number.

HE HAD to wait quite a while this time. He guessed Sheila was probably in bed. It was nearly one in the morning. After what seemed an eternity he finally got her. "Hello, hon."

Instantly she was wide awake. "Rex! What's happened?"

"I am now a murderer," he said, adding, "but a very privileged murderer, hon. I am out on bail and allowed to walk around, just so I don't stray too far." He told her about the girl Juanita and his experience with Train. "The guy scares me stiff," he said gloomily, "but I can't make up my mind whether he's the guy I'm after. Sometimes I think yes, sometimes I think no. Anyway he gave me a so-called tip and I think we'd better follow it through."

Sheila caught her breath. "Then you didn't quit! All the rest of it—all the things you said—that was just camouflage?"

"Look, hon," he said quietly, "things are beginning to break pretty fast. I can't get out of town myself, so I've got to trust somebody. You're the only one I could think of. Don't let me down, will you?"

"You should know me better than that, Rex."

"I should know everybody better than I do," he said stubbornly. "Trouble is, there're too many people in this thing and a careless word, even to someone you think is all right, may wreck the whole works. Don't talk, even to old man Leeds."

"Mr. Leeds is in the hospital, Rex. He may not live. All this trouble—"

"I know," he said. He made a bitter mouth. "Even God seems to be taking a hand in making it tougher. The river's flooding."

"What do you want me to do, Rex?"

"Lieutenant Escobar may get in touch with you some time after the banks open in the morning. We're checking up on Erin Rourke."

"Rourke!" she gasped. "Why, Rourke is on our side. His is one of the companies underwriting the job."

"Rourke don't own the company," McBride said grimly. "He's just an employee. He may be feathering his own nest at the expense of the others." He sighed. "Anyway, we're checking him, and while we're at it we might just as well check all the others too. You go see a stockbroker named Art Lawson and get the exact dates of this guy Train's short sales. Especially the first one. Find out who else has been in the market on the short end of Leeds & Leeds."

"You mean you've eliminated Carmichael and the Five Companies?"

"Hell, no. I'm not even sure it isn't Carmichael who's trying to eliminate me. I'm just playing all the angles I can, hon." He took a breath. "Incidentally, if you can't reach me by phone—if I don't call you before tomorrow night—you'd better get in touch with Colin Leeds up here. That is, if you locate anything."

"You're expecting more trouble, aren't you, Rex? You're in danger."

"A little," he admitted. He wasn't working on her sympathy; he just thought it wise to let her know how things stood. "I'll get by though, hon. You all right?"

"Of course."

"I'm crazy about your voice, hon."

"You're not so bad, yourself," she said. This time she let McBride break the connection. He felt that he was really going places. He felt, in fact, like a million dollars. He was actually pleasant to Engstrom when, a few minutes later, the hacker arrived with the gin. "Engie, old pal, you're a refuge in my hour of need."

Engstrom looked at him suspiciously. "You been drinking?"

"Nectar," McBride said. "Nectar of the gods, Engie."

"Me, I'll take gin," Engstrom said. He took some. McBride stared at a suspicious looking bulge in the guy's coat pocket. "I wondered what took you so long. You've been and gone and got yourself another gun, haven't you?"

Engstrom flushed. To cover his embarrassment he took another shot of gin. Then, like a kid with a secret, he grinned. "I been practicing," he confessed. "I been practicing my split-second draw. Look!" His split-second draw consumed nearly two minutes. The gun had become wedged in his pocket and he finally had to put the gin bottle down and use both hands.

McBride admired him elaborately. "I get it. The other guy is supposed to wait for you."

Engstrom glared. "You go to hell!"

McBRIDE picked up the phone. "Hi, toots, can you get me a lady by the name of Lou Queen?"

The operator sniffed. "If she's a lady I'm a gazelle!"

"All right, gazelle, get me Lou Queen." While he was waiting McBride reached out and took the bottle away from Engstrom. "If you were going to drink it all yourself you could just as well have stayed downstairs."

Engstrom sulkily began practicing his split-second draw.

McBride said, "Hello, Lou. Yes, I'm out. I don't know why but I am. No, I haven't beaten the rap." Her voice came to him, melodiously sympathetic. After a moment he said hesitantly, "Look, Lou, I don't want to put you on a spot or anything—"

"That's okay, Irish. What was it you wanted to know about— what we were discussing when those Beale heels busted in?"

"Yes."

"Juanita used to work for me," she said. "That was before she got a break with Bill Van. Some of my girls were still friendly with her and one of them happened to drop in. She was dead then. The gal came to me, scared to death. I told her to forget it."

"What time was this?"

"The gal saw you go into the place. She must have come out just as you drove up."

"Then she ought to be able to prove I didn't do the job."

"Except for the prints on the knife. The cops may think you're a fool, but you'd have a time convincing them you actually grabbed the sticker intending to pull it out. Did you?"

"No," McBride said. He explained how his prints happened to be where they were. "It's just one of those things, I guess."

"And I didn't help you any by lying, did I?"

McBride stiffened. Here was a brand new thought. Suppose Lou Queen had lied, knowing full well that the cops would immediately disprove her statement? People don't often lie unless there is something to cover up. Had the lady done her best to tighten the noose around McBride's neck? He said, "That's okay, Lou. Forget it." He waited, hoping she would mention the other thing—the miniature of herself and St. George Train. She didn't. He said, "Well, I'll be seeing you keed."

"Sure, Irish, any time."

He hung up. Another lead gone, he thought. He'd been hoping Lou Queen could point him to Juanita's killer. Instead of that, all she'd done was explain how she'd known Juanita was dead. He wasn't even sure the explanation itself was on the level. If it was, the girl who had seen him probably thought he was the murderer returning to the scene of the crime.

Engstrom had almost perfected his split-second draw. "Look!" he said exultantly. His hand flashed to his pocket. The gun stuck again. Getting it out this time he ripped his pocket.

McBride said, "Why don't you carry it in your teeth?" He put on his hat and topcoat. As an afterthought he shoved Engstrom's other gun in the waistband of his trousers and pulled his vest down over it. He disliked heavy guns in his pockets because they spoiled the hang of his clothes. Not that this arrangement was much better. He felt like a tired business man with a paunch. He thought the gun must surely be as obvious to an observer as it was to him, but he was disspirited anyway so it didn't make much difference. "Come on, pal. I've got to see a guy."

"Who?"

"Colin Leeds. Know where he lives?"

Engstrom said he did. He said, "You gonna knock him off?"

"Probably," McBride said. "If I don't, somebody else will and I'll get blamed for it anyway." He clicked off the lights before opening the hall door. There were no lurking assassins. They went down and got in Engstrom's cab and rode out to the Leeds' place.

THIS was a smaller bungalow than Carmichael's. Through a lighted front window McBride could see into the living room. There was a drafting board set up on horses and a bunch of maps on the walls and over in one corner there was a littered desk. McBride decided that if Colin Leeds had a wife he must have left her in Los Angeles. There was certainly no evidence of a woman's refining influence here. He rang the bell.

After a short wait Leeds opened the door. His eyes were bloodshot and he still carried himself as though he had the weight of the world on his shoulders. That wasn't all he was carrying, either. He had quite a nice edge on. He stank of gin and fresh limes.

"Hello, heel."

"Hello," McBride said, unoffended. "May I come in?"

"Why?"

"Because I want some information."

"To peddle to Carmichael?"

McBride said patiently, "I don't mind standing out here. If Carmichael himself should see me he wouldn't worry. I arranged things so he wouldn't."

Leeds' eyes steadied. "You told him you were coming to me?"

"I told him I might."

Leeds stepped aside. "Come in, McBride." They went into the cluttered front room. McBride pulled the window blinds. "On the porch I was not so good a target," he said. He turned and watched Leeds pouring another drink. "None for me, thanks."

"This is for me, thanks," Leeds said.

McBride's eyes smoldered. "You're almost as nasty as your father," he said. "Maybe you've reason to be. On the other hand, I haven't gotten all the breaks either."

"What do you want?"

"A little information about the various so-called accidents. You may not gain by giving me this, but you've certainly nothing to lose. Or have you?"

Leeds put his glass down on the drafting board, careless of the drawing spread out there. "Is that a crack?"

"Not unless you care to take it that way." McBride lit a cigarette. "Some of the things that happened must be traceable to certain men. I don't mean that anything more than carelessness could be proven, but I'd like to find one or two of the careless ones."

"So would I," Leeds said. "What's your object in this—to cover up Carmichael still further?"

McBride lost his temper. "Damn it, if I were in as strong with Carmichael as you think I am, and if he's the brains behind this business I wouldn't have to come to you, would I?"

"You could be trying to find out how much I know."

"If you knew anything—if you could prove anything—you'd have acted on it before this. Why don't you be your age, Leeds? I'm trying to help you. I've been trying all along, only I had to play it my way for a while."

Leeds suddenly slumped in a chair. "I'm a sick man, McBride. My father is a wreck. We're about ready to turn over the job to the Five Companies. So, as you say, I haven't a thing to lose by giving you all the information you want."

"That's what I thought," McBride said.

Leeds picked up his drink, looked at it, put it down again. Apparently he knew it wasn't solving his problem to get swacked to the eyes. He began talking, heavily, without inflection. "Accidents are nothing new in this game. Everybody has 'em. For a time, that's all we thought it was, just a run of bad luck. By the time we woke up and started checking back we discovered that two of the men who might have been bribed had quit and disappeared. Another was found dead, apparently beaten to death for his money. Then there was the man Swiggart. We had nothing on him. The board of inquiry really worked him over but nothing came of it."

"So you fired him."

Leeds nodded. "Now he's dead too."

"Then there's no one else I might get hold of?"

Leeds smiled tiredly. "There's old Tony Garcia. The only thing is, Tony had an arm blown off in the explosion and I hardly think he'd have arranged that. He's retired on a pension."

"I think I'll have a talk with Tony anyway," McBride said. "Mind giving me his address?"

"It won't do any good." Leeds had reached the point where nothing would do any good. He was beaten. "I tell you he swore to me on his knees that he didn't know how it happened. Besides, there's his own arm."

"I'll still take the address," McBride said. Getting it, he put on his hat and went out to the hall. At the door he turned. "About the Five Companies, I wouldn't if I were you. Hold off for another day or two at least. I'll tell Carmichael you're thinking about it"

Leeds stared at him unbelievingly. "You'd do that?" Hot anger flooded his face. "Why, damn you—" He swung a fist at McBride's chin. McBride caught him by the arms, held him still. "You fool, I know what I'm doing. If Carmichael thinks you're licked he won't try anything else, will he?"

Leeds went limp. "That's so," he said dully. Hope flickered in his bloodshot eyes. "I don't understand you, McBride, but—"

McBride said, "I don't understand myself half the time." He went out to the porch muttering something about an enigma. "That's what I am, the great Irish enigma."

HE PAUSED at sight of Engstrom sitting there disconsolately on the steps. "Why so sad, Viking?"

Engstrom got up. He looked haggard. "You remember when I tore my pocket up in your room?"

"Sure."

"Well, I put my gun in it, see? And now it's—"

McBride's ribald laughter echoed in the quiet street. "Don't tell me, Engie. Let me guess. It did a split-second draw all by itself!"

"Well, in a way, yes."

"And you can't find it?"

"No."

"It serves you right," McBride said callously. "You filched it from under the nose of the Board of Trade anyway." Ignoring Engstrom's plea to help him find the gun he went out and climbed in the cab. They rolled back toward town. They were less than a block away from the Grand National when the shooting began. There was a staccato burst of machine-gun fire, apparently inside the hotel itself. The heavier, deeper boom of a .45 punctuated the rattle at intervals and finally one of the front windows went out in a great clatter. Engstrom braked to a halt.

McBRIDE sat there for a moment, reaching calmly for the gun under the waistband of his trousers, then he went grimly into action.

They were still a good hundred yards away. McBride slammed the door open, climbed out. Two men debouched from the hotel, ran toward a gray sedan in which there was a third man. Pedestrians huddled together on the sidewalks, immovable, paralyzed. The men got in the car and it shot away. McBride knelt, aiming carefully, steadying his bucking gun with his left hand. The rear window of the sedan disappeared in a silver shower. The sedan disappeared too. McBride got up and ran the rest of the way to the hotel.

They were helping the fat hotel dick to a chair. One of his arms was shattered and there was a streak of blood on his face. A second man lay on the floor in front of the desk. He was beyond help. You could tell it by the way he sprawled there, face down, inert. A little pool of blood leaked out from under his chin. He wore a natty dark blue Chesterfield and there was a derby near one outflung hand. McBride didn't have to turn him over to know who he was. He was Train's gunsel.

Three white-faced clerks bobbed up from behind the desk. Out in the street a siren wailed. McBride looked at the gaping safe. "My envelope, boys?"

"That's gone too!" one of them gasped. "They took it with the rest."

CHAPTER XIX

TWO-WAY RIDE

THE LOBBY OF the Grand National was beginning to assume a more normal aspect. The body of Mr. Train's gunsel had been removed and a porter mopped industriously at the spot where he had lain. The fat house-dick was being treated in the hotel's infirmary. Across the shattered front window a tarpaulin had been stretched pending the arrival of the glaziers in the morning. It was just two o'clock.

Chief Beale and his paunchy brother Harry were interrogating witnesses. There was a profusion of these. The bar did a land-office business. McBride sat quietly in a U-shaped club chair near the desk. It had been established that the dead gunsel was one of the three men who had held up the hotel. His was the only identification on which all agreed. He had been right there. Even eye-witnesses couldn't miss. The fat house dick, appearing unexpectedly on the scene, had surprised everyone, including himself, by hauling out his gun and banging away. It was he who had shot the gunsel. The machine-gunner had shot the house dick. McBride wondered how it was possible for a machine gun to do so little damage. The house dick's injuries consisted of one shattered arm. He remembered that St. George Train had known the man very well indeed, though apparently he hadn't known him well enough to apprise him in advance of the intended hostilities. This struck McBride as very curious, because the gray man had always given him the impression of efficiency raised to the highest power.

The bandit car had not been located. No one was sure whether it had or had not carried license plates. McBride himself couldn't have sworn to it, and he had been right out there in the middle of the street shooting at the rear of the car. He resolved never again to revile an eye-witness to anything.

Two dicks came through the front door and spoke to the brothers Beale. Chief Beale went out with them. Harry moved ponderously across the expanse of carpet till his big feet almost trod on McBride's. "Who did it, shamus?"

McBride looked at him. "You really want to know?"

"I want to know."

"Well," McBride said, "my guess is Train."

Beale made disparaging sounds with his fat lips. "You ought to be ashamed, shamus. After all Mr. Train did for you."

McBride said, "Naturally I don't expect you to arrest him. The king can do no wrong. You just asked and I told you."

Beale reached down leisurely and got McBride by the shoulders and hauled him to his feet. "What makes you think it was Train?"

"The guy in the Chesterfield was Train's gunsel. Train told me so, right after he had me sprung. Also, Train was right at my elbow when I got my dough from the clerk to square the five-grand bond." McBride shrugged out from under Beale's grip. "None of this means anything, of course."

"How much dough you have left at the desk?"

"Three grand," McBride said bitterly. "The hotel management talks as though they don't intend to do anything about it."

Beale wiped sweat from his upper lip. "Train wouldn't be interested in three grand."

McBride didn't think so either. Not in an ordinary three grand. He thought Train might have been interested in the two hundred-dollar bills, though. He didn't say this. He said, "The hoods got other stuff beside mine."

"Train still wouldn't be interested."

*"I think he passed out," Scarface
said, peering down at McBride.*

McBride sighed. "Perhaps you're right."

"Funny thing about that gunsel," Beale said casually. His small eyes rested obliquely on McBride. "He had some rifle cartridges on him."

"Is that so?"

"Unh-hunh. Another funny thing—you remember the hardware salesman?"

McBride did. He still felt like hell about the hardware salesman. Beale said triumphantly, "Well, sir, the slugs in this gunsel's pockets were the same kind that did for the salesman." His case-hardened eyes steadied on McBride's face. "Not only that, they were the same as the one that made that cute little bullet hole in your window."

"Oh, you found that, did you?"

Beale shrugged. "We ain't so dumb. The house dick reported in and we came over and dug the slug out of the wall."

"That makes it very convenient," McBride said. "Your murders just seem to solve themselves, don't they?" He watched the slow color climb up into Beale's moon face. "You find the rifle?"

"Not yet."

"You might ask Train, if he has it."

Beale's eyes got ugly. "You lay off of Train, shamus. I told you he wouldn't be interested in a nickel-snatching heist like this. Lay off, hear me?"

McBride set fire to a cigarette, snapped the match at a potted palm. "The case is closed as far as I'm concerned."

"That's better," Beale said. "You keep on feeling that way and maybe we won't throw you back in the can for a while."

McBride let smoke dribble out of his mouth. "It would be nice if you could pin Juanita's murder on that gunsel too. Not that I don't think he gunned the hardware salesman. Probably he did."

He watched Beale lumber off.

MR. FRANZ CHARLES hurried through the revolving doors, stared resentfully at the litter of glass being swept up, spotted McBride and nodded almost imperceptibly at the mezzanine. He went up the stairs. After a moment McBride went up the stairs, too.

Charles was wearing holes in one of the Chinese rugs. Otherwise the mezzanine was deserted. Charles was his usual immaculate self, though his habitual austerity was now shaded with unmistakable signs of nervousness. "I just heard about it, McBride. How are you fixed for money?"

"I've still got a few dollars left," McBride said. He didn't mention that he had augmented his own diminishing roll by robbing Erin Rourke. "Enough to hold me, I think."

Mr. Charles allowed a gleam of hope to show in his bleak eyes. "Then you're really accomplishing something, eh?" He rubbed his hands gently together. "That's fine. That's fine."

"I ought to have something definite by tomorrow evening at the latest," McBride said. "You keep this under your hat, understand? Don't tell anybody."

Charles nodded. "I've done my best to avoid you since I've been here. The meeting at the desk was a little unfortunate, but it couldn't be helped. It was, I may say, your own fault. You've rather gone out of your way to cultivate Miss Ford and she quite naturally spoke to you."

"She's certainly made up for the lapse since," McBride said. He leered at his employer. "I sympathize with you, having to put up with a secretary like her."

Mr. Charles frowned. "You're impertinent, McBride. I told you before that she is my secretary and nothing more."

"I know you did. If I were in your position I'd lie too."

Charles shrugged impatiently. "This is getting us nowhere, McBride. Think what you choose and be damned to you." He looked down at the crowded lobby. "This robbery affect your case any?"

"It didn't accomplish its purpose, if that's what you mean."

"I'm glad to hear it," Charles said briskly. "Morals aside, I believe you were the right man for this job, McBride."

"Morals aside, I like you too," McBride said. "You staying over the weekend?"

Charles said he was. "I saw Leeds for a short time this evening but he'd been drinking and I decided to put our conference over till tomorrow."

"A good idea," McBride said. "I saw the guy too." He tugged at his hat. "Well, we'd better not be seen talking together again. If I need you I'll let you know." He left Charles there on the balcony and descended to the lobby just in time to run into Engstrom, who was looking for him.

"Look," Engstrom said, "I found my gun!"

McBride cursed him. "Damn it, I sent you after a Mexican named Tony Garcia and you come back with a lost gun!"

Engstrom was profoundly hurt. "That's gratitude for you. I already located Garcia before I found my gun, and so then I thought—"

"Where?"

"Right in the seat of my own hack. Can you beat it?"

"Not the gun, you fool! Garcia."

"Oh."

McBride, exasperated to the point of mayhem, grabbed a handful of Engstrom's coat lapels. "Look, Engie, let's please—pul-lease—forget your rod for a minute. Let's talk about this Mex. Where is he?"

"At the Natividad," Engstrom said sullenly. "I went out to his house—you oughta see the dump—and some fat dame told me where he was, so I went there. He's playin' faro."

"You didn't say anything to him?"

"No."

"Then how'd you know it was him?"

"He's only got one arm, ain't he?" Engstrom demanded. "Besides I asked a couple of guys."

"I might have known," McBride grated. "I might have known!" He hurled Engstrom from him and crossed the lobby as though he were in a very great hurry. He was still in a hurry when he entered the Club Natividad, but he was too late. The faro bank had plenty of customers but none of them was a one-armed Mexican.

McBRIDE moved swiftly but not conspicuously about the packed casino. Smoke hung in thick layers up against the ceiling and the lights were hot and bright. The sickish-sweet smell of stale liquor and sweat and perfume was overpowering, nauseous, and the drone of voices was like the echo of surf in a cave. Up on the balcony over the dining room entrance William Van, the very fat and allegedly genial host of the Natividad, surveyed his domain with a fishy eye.

McBride went into the lavatory. Garcia was not here either. There was nobody here but a drunk who retched miserably in one of the stalls. In the opposite wall there was a door, bolted on the inside. McBride opened it, went out into a stygian alley whose only light filtered in from the cross streets. The rear wall of the Natividad was a dark expanse of brick, unbroken as far as McBride could see, though there must have been other outlets because he stumbled over a pile of refuse cans. The clatter of a lid on the cobbles was deafening. He almost missed the faint cry that came from the other side of the heaped-up cans.

"Mercy of God, *señor!*" A horrible choking sound followed this and the hackles rose on McBride's neck. He fumbled a match out of his pocket, struck it. Pale yellow light illumined the face of an aged, grizzled Mexican. He had but one arm. An eight-inch gash in his abdomen gaped redly, obscenely, and his one gnarled hand clawed at it. His eyes were closed.

McBride's match went out. He dropped down beside the man on the cobbles. "Garcia!"

"Si, *señor?*" It was very weak and there was the sound of blood in it. "Mother of God—"

McBride thought he had died. "Garcia, who did this to you?" He struck another match. The old man's eyes were glazing and new blood welled on his lips as he fought for breath. "Beel, do not do thees thing." He screamed. "Beel!"

McBride put his mouth down close. "Which Beale?"

Garcia didn't answer. He couldn't answer, because he was dead. McBride, hunkered down on his heels, stunned for a moment, was in no position to ward off the noose that settled over his head. He scarcely knew it was there before it was jerked tight about his throat and he sprawled flat on his back. A vague shape loomed over him and something heavy and very hard clunked against his chin. He went out as completely as the match he had held.

AFTER a while he roused a little and realized that he was on the floor of a moving car. He could smell the raw fumes of gasoline. The constricting wire or cord was still about his throat but by taking it slow and easy he found that he could breath without choking to death. There was another body beside him, inert as his own, and he guessed that probably this was the Mexican, Garcia. Something that felt like a pair of feet pinioned McBride face down on the floor and presumably the owner of the feet was on the seat, holding the other end of the wire. It moved whenever the feet moved.

McBride worked his hands under him, feeling for the gun in his waistband. It wasn't there any more. He lay quietly, afraid that any sudden move would decapitate him. He was almost sure now that the noose was made of wire, probably picture wire. He remembered that a long time ago he had hung a picture and that picture wire was very strong. He'd ruined his mother's shears, cutting it.

They weren't moving very fast. McBride knew this because he could hear switch engines in the yards, and the yards were less than half a mile from the Club Natividad. Presently they jolted over a series of tracks and the car halted. "Okay?" This voice would be the driver's. The guy cleaning his feet on McBride's back said, "Yeah," and there was the sound of opening doors. The inert figure beside McBride was hauled out.

"Number 4 ought to be along pretty quick," the driver said. He grunted a little as though he were lifting a dead weight. He got back in the car. "Yuh know, that's what I like about a shiv. It don't leave no marks a train couldn't."

"Yeah."

McBride tried moving a little as the car got under way. The noose jerked tight, shutting off his wind. "Quiet, you!" He relaxed. He wondered why they didn't kill him and put him on the tracks too. Again the car halted. This time the guy at the other end of the halter really put his mind on his work. Waves of blackness rolled around McBride's head, blackness studded here and there with bright shooting darts. He wasn't totally unconscious; he could feel them lifting and carrying him, but he couldn't do much about it. He was thrown heavily to a floor harder than that of the tonneau. The pressure on his throat decreased. His first tortured breath was laden with the unforgettable smell of a box car. The rumble of the door was like distant thunder.

For a moment he thought he was alone. Then a flashlight

stabbed him in the face. It was focused in a broad beam, so that
by slitting his eyes he could see past it, see the interior of the
car. He had never seen either of the two guys before. It would
have been all right with him if he never saw them again. He
lay there, blinking, and presently he put up his hands and loosened the wire.

The gorilla with the scarred face said, "Hi, tough guy."

"Hi." McBride tried to sit up and the other guy came over
and kicked him in the side. McBride grabbed the guy's leg and
sat him on his bottom. Scarface kicked him in the chin. He lay
quietly for a moment. Scarface got down on his knees, strad-
dling McBride's chest, and worked the noose around till the
loose end was in front. He wrapped the loose end around his
fist. "Take off his shoes, Petey."

Petey took off McBride's shoes. He said incredulously, "His
socks is real silk!" He lit a match and touched fire to one of the
socks. This did McBride's foot, inside the sock, little or no good.
He yelled.

Scarface tightened up on the wire a trifle. "Go ahead, yell
your head off!"

"What do you want?" McBride croaked.

"The dough."

"What dough?"

"Go ahead, Petey," Scarface said. "Light the other foot."

A match flared. "Hey, wait!" McBride yelled. "I'm serious."

"So are we," Scarface said. "We want them two C-notes."

"I don't know what you're talking about."

Scarface sighed. "This is gonna hurt you more'n it does me,
pal. Light up, Petey." As the match crackled Scarface tightened
up on the wire. He also tightened his knees about McBride's
middle. Flame seared the right foot and McBride let out an
agonized yelp and went limp. It was hell but he didn't even jerk.

"I think he passed out," Scarface said. He leaned over, his
face so close that McBride could smell the gin on his breath.
McBride had to move his left hand less than six inches to get

the gun under the guy's arm. He shot him three times in the stomach.

Petey cursed. "Damn it, what'd you do that for?" Then he saw that it was McBride, not Scarface who had done the shooting, and he hauled his own rod and almost shot McBride's ear off. McBride, cumbered with the bulky Scarface and shooting left-handed, was in no position to be choosey. He just squeezed the trigger in Petey's general direction. It was Petey's misfortune that the slug hit him in the throat and ranged upward. He'd been dead three seconds by the time he hit the floor.

McBRIDE rolled sluggishly out from under his burden. He almost choked himself to death. Scarface still had the wire wrapped around his wrist. McBride gasped, "You would, hunh?" and slugged Scarface with the gun. The guy didn't even grunt. McBride, surprised at this, looked closer and saw that the eyes were wide open, starey. Scarface wouldn't care if he was slugged all night. He was beyond caring about anything any more.

After a while McBride got the wire free. Presently he stood up. Immediately he wished he hadn't. A blister the size of an egg burst. He thought for a minute he was going to die, but he didn't. He got down on his knees and crawled over and got the flashlight and started the messy job of searching his victims. There was nothing on either of them that even told him their names.

He sat there for a time, thinking. It was quite evident that the two hundred-dollar notes were of great importance to somebody. It was known that McBride possessed them; that he had gotten them from the girl Juanita. Undoubtedly she had been made to talk before they killed her. And the raid on the hotel safe having failed to produce the wanted bills, it was supposed that McBride had them somewhere else. St. George Train, of course, had seen McBride separate two bills from the sheaf in the envelope. This pointed directly to Train as the instigator of the raid; also there was Train's dead gunsel left on the scene.

Against all this you had the fact that Train could have killed or kidnapped McBride at any time immediately following his release from jail. There was also the matter of the murder of old Tony Garcia in the alley back of the Club Natividad. Why had these two gorillas, here in the car with McBride, bothered to remove the Mexican and mask his death as a railroad accident? The answer to this was, obviously, that somebody didn't want him found there. He'd been dumped temporarily, and the two hoods had then gone to get a car. Returning, they had stumbled on McBride. He disregarded their interest in the two bills for a moment. The point was, who would be most interested in getting the dead Mexican off the Natividad premises? The owner, maybe? William Van?

Considering this possibility McBride was struck by an odd thought. How about "Beel" as a Mexican's pronunciation of "Bill" instead of "Beale"? Had Garcia known William Van well enough to call him "Bill"? It sounded screwy, but it was a possibility, at that. One thing sure about this case, you weren't in any danger of running out of ideas.

McBride deliberately broke two more blisters and almost fainted. Not far away a locomotive whistled. It sounded like a mainliner. McBride shivered. After a while he put on his shoes. Then, sorting his own belongings from those of Scarface and Petey, he slid the door open.

The car outside was a gray sedan. Its rear window was shattered and McBride thought that undoubtedly it was the car used in the Grand National heist. He limped over and shone the flash on the registration. The car belonged to Carmichael, president of the Five Companies.

CHAPTER XX

SUSPECTS ON PARADE

ENGSTROM, OPENING THE door of McBride's room, vented a startled oath. "Excuse me, lady!" Attempting to back out he tramped on one of McBride's sore feet. "Excuse me, pal, but this is the wrong room."

McBride cursed him. "Will you keep off my dogs?" He looked over Engstrom's shoulder. Miss Ford waved at him from the bed. She wasn't in it; she was just on it. She had been asleep and had pulled the extra blanket over her for warmth, but McBride saw with relief that she was fully dressed.

She smiled at him. "Hello, Rex."

Engstrom began a hasty retreat. McBride said, "Wait, mug," and followed him down the hall a little way. "Look, Engie, whoever you talked to at the Natividad knew you were working with me. Be careful, you dope. I'd hate to find you in an alley like I did Tony Garcia."

Engstrom wet his lips. "If you want me I'll be down in the boiler room." He disappeared around an ell in the corridor. McBride retraced his steps to his own room. Miss Ford was still on the bed. He closed the door, staring at her with sombre eyes. "How did you get in?"

"A bellboy loaned me his key."

He removed his coat and hat, sat down and began taking off his shoes. "For fifteen bucks a day I might just as well stayed in the lobby."

"This is much cozier," Miss Ford yawned. She swung her legs off the bed. "Aren't you glad to see me, Rex?"

"Sure," he said. "Sure." The remnants of one of his socks had stuck to a broken blister. He wouldn't have been interested in Garbo at the moment.

Miss Ford caught her breath. "Oh, my dear, what have they done to you?"

"They're great jokers around here," McBride said. "This is the Palos Verde conception of the well-known hot foot." He limped painfully into the bath.

She followed him, went to the medicine cabinet. Included by the management at no extra charge were a score of advertising samples. Miss Ford selected a couple of these, saturated a bath towel with steaming hot water. "Sit there," she directed. She knelt at McBride's feet.

He looked fondly down at her bowed head. "A modern Magdalene."

She said, "How do you ever expect to go to heaven, Rex?"

"Did I say I did?" He sucked in a breath as she removed the towel. After a moment he said, "You're a beautiful tramp, Kay."

She smeared lotion, then ointment on the soles of his feet. Quite suddenly she lifted her head and he saw that she was crying. "You've no right to call me that, Rex, just because I— we—"

He bent and kissed her. "I'm sorry, hon."

She wrapped gauze loosely around his feet. "I suppose there's no good telling you you'd better keep off these for a while."

"Oh, I don't know," he said. "There's not much I can do till the banks open in the morning anyway." He went in and sat on the bed. Presently, when she came in too, he said, "You used to be a nurse, didn't you?"

Her blue eyes were startled. "How did you know?"

"A little birdie," he said. "Not the same one that told me you carry a rod when you search guys' apartments."

Unexpectedly she laughed. "So that stewardess was another one of your conquests! My, Rex, and she so young!"

He flushed darkly. "That's what comes of the flower habit. She's a nice kid. She just didn't understand, is all." His sultry eyes rested on her very blue ones. "What did you expect to find?"

She wrinkled her nose. All trace of her tears was gone. She was beautiful. "After all," she said, "you started it. Who was it I found searching *my* apartment?"

"Me?" he offered.

"You." She sat beside him. Presently she turned a little, cupped his chin in her two hands and kissed him on the mouth. "We had quite an evening, remember?"

His eyes glowed. "Could I ever forget it?"

"A girl can't be too careful," she said. "I thought I'd better find out a little more about you before I really went overboard."

"And the rod?"

She shrugged. "You can't ever tell what you'll find in a closet these days."

He chuckled. "And that's a fact, babe." Yawning, he began laying out fresh pajamas. "Mind if I catch a little shut-eye, hon?"

She looked at him. He said, "Hell's bells, I'm tired! Besides, there's always Mr. Franz Charles."

She flushed.

"Don't be nasty, Rex. Charles is my employer, nothing else."

He yawned widely. "I'd like to be able to employ you, babe."

She went to the door. Hand on the knob she turned. "You evil-minded Casanova," she said. Then she was gone.

GRINNING, McBride picked up the phone and called Carmichael. He couldn't make up his mind whether Carmichael was irritated at being called in the middle of the night or was sore about something else. "You'd better come up here, pal. Time's a'wasting and I've tried two or three times to get you."

"You're damned right I'll be up there!" Carmichael said.

"You're no more anxious to see me than I am to see you." He banged up the phone.

McBride looked at his own instrument with a puzzled frown. Finally he shrugged and donned his pajamas and climbed into bed. The perfume of Miss Ford still lingered on the top blanket. McBride tried to consider Miss Ford as just another pawn in the game but it was very difficult. She was almost beginning to overshadow Sheila. He jacked a shell into the chamber of his automatic and laid the gun beside him under the covers. Then, pillows propped behind his head, he lay there and smoked and thought and wished he wasn't so sleepy.

Perhaps twenty minutes went by and there was still no Carmichael. McBride was just about to get up and lock the door and call it a day when the knock came. He relaxed, right arm under the covers. "Come in."

Carmichael came in. His lean dark face was haggard and the close-set eyes were a trifle bloodshot. He looked as though he'd been on a two-weeks' binge. He kept his right hand in his overcoat, and McBride, observant of such things, was convinced that the bulge wasn't all fist. Carmichael reached his left hand behind him and closed the door.

McBride said, "If that's a gun you've got, you needn't be afraid of me, pal."

"Afraid!" Carmichael laughed harshly. "How much money have you given my wife, McBride?"

"Who, me?" In spite of himself McBride was startled. He half rose. Carmichael's impatient gesture pushed him down again. He said earnestly, "So help me, all I've done is buy your wife a dinner!"

"I heard you," Carmichael rasped. "I overheard you promising her money. And I found out this evening that she's in over her head with Billy Van at the Natividad. She's lost thousands besides, too."

"Not any of my thousands, she hasn't."

Carmichael started to shake. "You're lying. She told me. I made her tell me!"

There's a blonde for you, McBride thought. What does she mean, sending her husband after me instead of that guy Rourke? Aloud he said, "Look, pal, you've got a gun in your pocket. I've got one pointing right at you. Which one of us do you think will get hurt?"

Carmichael looked uncertainly at the bed. Finally he decided that McBride wasn't bluffing and took his hand out of his pocket. He sat heavily in a chair, avoiding McBride's eyes. "I guess I'm a fool to care about her."

McBride thought so too, but he didn't say this. He was actually sorry for the guy, but his main concern at the moment was to advantage himself through this unexpected development. "I saw Colin Leeds. He's ready to sell to your outfit."

"Is he?"

"You're not exactly enthusiastic," McBride said. "Isn't that what you've wanted all along?"

Carmichael looked at him dully. "Of course. I appreciate what you've done, McBride." He made a bitter mouth. "Even though you and my wife—"

McBride yelled, "I'm not interested in your wife! All she's done is maybe peddle a few of your business secrets to certain parties." His eyes were very bright under half-lowered lids. "I give you credit for not telling her enough to put your neck in a sling."

Carmichael roused. "What's that?"

McBride said, "I ought to pump you full of lead for trying to have me knocked off."

Carmichael really looked at him this time. "I don't understand you, McBride. What's the idea of all this double talk? I haven't tried to have you knocked off."

"The cops will find your car."

"I hope they do," Carmichael said. "It's taking them long enough."

McBride sighed. "So you reported it stolen?"

"Of course. Isn't that the usual procedure?"

"That's the trouble," McBride said wearily. "It's the usual procedure, even when the owner knows what the car's going to be used for."

Carmichael rubbed a hand over his eyes. "I still don't get it."

McBride decided that this was probably a fact. Carmichael was and had been too emotionally upset to do a good job of acting. He said, "Your car was used in a heist tonight, or rather this morning. It was used to transport a corpse down to the railroad yards. I know, because I rode with the corpse."

"No!"

"A fact," McBride nodded. "I'm just telling you in case you want to do a little housecleaning. With all this killing we're going to have some law in here pretty quick. Some real law, I mean."

Carmichael wet his lips. "See here, McBride, was what—what you said about my wife the truth? You were just bribing her to get a line on me?"

McBride decided to be a gentleman at all costs. "Cross my heart, that's all."

THERE was a knock on the door. Without waiting to be invited Erin Rourke bounced in. "I heard voices, McBride—" He saw Carmichael. "Oh, hello, Jack!"

McBride said, "You two know each other?"

"Of course," Rourke beamed. "I hope to shout we do. I wrote Carmichael up myself for his first big policy. How's the wife, Jack?"

"She's—fine," Carmichael said. He looked at McBride. "I think I'd better be running along." He went to the door. "About the other, you ought to know by this time that I'm in the clear." He nodded pleasantly enough at Rourke. "Drop around and see us some time, Erin. Any time." He let himself out.

McBride picked up the phone. He was so mad he was

shaking. Mrs. Carmichael answered almost immediately. "Listen," McBride said, "I'm sending your husband back to you thinking you're just unfortunate. What's that? No, you're not sorry. You're just scared to death. And let me tell you something else. If I ever hear of you stepping over the line again I'll come back and kill you with my bare hands!" He banged the phone down.

Rourke looked virtuous. "Who was that?"

McBride glared at him. "Your paramour. She damned near got me killed! And as for you—" He hauled the gun out from under the covers.

Rourke paled. "Now see here, Rex—"

"Yah! How anybody—even you—could go for a blonde, especially *that* blonde!" He pointed the gun at Rourke's middle. "What have you got in those three deposit boxes?"

"So it *was* you!" Rourke was disillusioned. "After all we've been to each other, too." His baby mouth looked as though he were going to cry but his eyes were bright, probing. "You heel!"

McBride shrugged. "As long as I've admitted something I didn't do—" He broke off, thinking darkly of Mrs. Carmichael. "Sure, I conked you." He lifted the gun. "Also, I just asked you a question. You don't have to answer. I'll have a report on the boxes as soon as the banks open anyway."

Rourke covered his face with his hands. His shoulders shook. He peeked at McBride through spread fingers. "Can you keep a secret?"

"I'm tired keeping secrets," McBride said sullenly. "Not that there ever were any secrets. I feel like I'd been walking through this case naked."

Rourke made a great pretense of candor. "Well, I'll tell you about those boxes, Rex. They're full of dough." He shuddered as McBride jerked the gun at him. "No, honestly, it's clean dough. Or almost clean, anyway. I've been converting a lot of my stuff into cash."

"Why? Chiseling on your wife, hunh?"

Rourke managed to look scared and indignant at the same time. "She's getting the divorce, isn't she? You want me to sacrifice my dough as well as my honor?"

"Your honor! A lot you know about honor."

"That Community Property law!" Rourke wailed. "They take half of everything a guy's got!" He looked pleadingly at McBride. "You won't tell?"

McBride said, "I'll plaster your name all over the front pages if you pull any more fast ones. And you keep away from Mrs. Carmichael, too!"

Rourke bobbed his round head violently. "You bet." He pretended to ignore the gun and edged toward the door. "What's the matter with Charles? What's he so sore about?"

"Maybe you've been playing around with *his* wife."

"He hasn't any."

"Well, then," McBride hazarded, "maybe he's worried about Leeds & Leeds. I'm glad to know that *you* are holding up so well."

Rourke spread pudgy hands. "But I'm not! I'm practically a nervous wreck. That's what I wanted to see Charles about—only they won't call him on the phone. Said he left orders not to be disturbed. So I thought"—Rourke looked sly—"well, knowing you, Rex, I thought maybe you were still working on the case."

McBride just looked at him. Rourke said plaintively, "It's that guy Train. He gives me the jeebies. Everywhere I go I seem to run into him."

"I'll take care of Train," McBride said.

THE PHONE rang. McBride answered it. Los Angeles was calling. Presently a crisp, authoritative voice said, "Mr. McBride? This is the County Hospital. We have a concussion case here and the patient keeps asking for you."

McBride's heart almost stopped beating. He ran a tongue over dry lips. "Who—who is it?"

"A girl named Hope Sullivan."

McBride's lips moved as though he might be praying. "How did it happen?"

"She was picked up just outside the airport. Slugged, apparently for her money. We haven't been able to get a thing out of her except your name and the fact that you were somewhere in Palos Verde."

"She's a plane stewardess. The officials of the line—"

"They've been notified. We just thought you ought to know the girl is calling for you."

McBride groaned. "Look, she's not going to—?"

"Die? Oh, no, we'll pull her out of it eventually. Only thing is, we don't know how long it will be. Perhaps if you could see her it would help."

"Listen," McBride said, "this may sound heartless to you but I just can't make it. Not right now, anyway. Keep in touch with me; let me know the minute she is able to talk. And incidentally I'll be responsible for all charges."

"That's all right, Mr. McBride."

McBride lowered his voice, put his lips very close to the mouthpiece. "One other thing—there may be people in to see her. Don't leave her unguarded a minute. Not a minute, understand?"

"You mean she's in danger of further attack?"

"I don't mean anything else," McBride said. Presently he cradled the phone and looked at Rourke. "What the hell are you waiting for?"

"Nothing," Rourke said meekly. "Nothing at all." He went out hastily. McBride called the operator downstairs. "Listen, toots, get hold of a florist. I want some flowers wired to a gal named Hope Sullivan in the County Hospital in L.A. I want the best flowers money will—"

"You know what time it is?"

"I don't even care!" McBride yelled. "You want that skunk coat or don't you?"

"Yes, Mr. McBride. I will see what I can do."

He replaced the phone gently. Then, like a man treading on eggs, he got up and went over and locked the door and braced a chair under the knob. He rolled the dresser across the communicating door. He climbed back into bed. After a while he even went to sleep. It wasn't a very restful sleep, though. He kept dreaming about Train and the fat guy, William Van, and about a little stewardess who looked quite a lot like Sheila Mason. Once he roused and reached for the phone in the darkness, thinking he would call Sheila. Then he thought that it would be a shame to wake her again. Faint light filtered in around the edge of the window drapes. It was nearly dawn. McBride went back to sleep.

CHAPTER XXI

DIRTY LINEN

TRAIN CAME IN a few minutes after ten. McBride was breakfasting in his room. He was newly shaved and dressed and on the whole looked pretty good. His feet were the worst. They were killing him. He had visions of blood poisoning.

Train was his usual immaculate self. The only other guy McBride knew that wore his clothes so well was Franz Charles, who had a couple of inches on McBride and was not so thick in the body. Train said, "Good morning, McBride." He had the musical, slightly pontifical tone of a bishop.

McBride waved at a bottle of sherry on the dresser. "Drink?"

"So you remembered, eh?" Train was politely pleased. He laid his hat and stick on the bed and poured himself a careful three fingers of the wine. He sipped this, eyeing McBride over the rim of his glass. "You have an excellent memory, my friend."

"About you I have," McBride said gloomily. He kept his right hand near the crumpled napkin on the table. "Couple of things I wanted to ask you, Train, before I went any farther."

"Yes?"

McBride gulped the last of his coffee. "Yes. Mind letting me see that trick dollar you carry?"

"Why?"

"It'll help me decide something."

"Very well," Train said. Thumb and forefinger dipped in a vest pocket and came out with the silver dollar. He tossed it. McBride caught it in his left hand, looked at it. It wasn't any trick dollar. It was exactly like any other silver dollar McBride had ever seen. He tossed it back. "Thanks."

Train smiled politely. "And what does that prove?"

"I don't know." McBride shrugged impatiently. "I can't explain my hunches always. It's just that I've met tinhorns with composite coins, either all heads or all tails. I wondered if you were like that."

Train put his dollar away. "And the other question, McBride?"

"The gunsel you said was yours. The one that got himself fogged in the heist last night."

"He was just mine temporarily," Train said. "Ordinarily I don't need gunhands. When I do I hire one."

McBride stood up. He lifted the napkin and without the slightest embarrassment picked up the gun and shoved it in the waistband of his pants. "Let's go see William Van."

"All right," Train said. They went down and got in Engstrom's cab and rode across town to the only apartment building in the city that had over five stories. This one had ten. It was quite a place. In the lobby a sleek young man reached for the telephone. Train lifted an eyebrow. "Do you have to announce us?"

The young man said no. He said it hastily, as though the word might be choking him. "Whatever you say, Mr. Train."

"Thank you," Train said. They used the automatic elevator to the tenth floor. In the corridor two men loitered, arguing desultorily over last night's card at the stadium. They didn't seem to be going any place. "Hello, boys," Train said pleasantly. They pretended they were waiting for the elevator. "Hello, Mr. Train."

Train rang the buzzer on the door of Number 15. They had to wait a little while. He didn't ring again, just waited. The two men were waiting too. They were arguing quite heatedly now.

PRESENTLY William Van opened the door. Van was not happy to see them. His triple chins were unshaven and the pouches under his fishy eyes were dark blue, as though he hadn't slept well. A quilted satin dressing gown did nothing whatever toward slenderizing his gross tonnage. He nodded without pleasure at McBride, said, "Hello, boss," to Mr. Train.

They all went into the combination living room and office. There seemed to be no one else in the apartment. Van slopped rye whisky into a tumbler, pushed the bottle across the desk. McBride poured a moderate drink. Neither bothered to make an occasion of it. They just drank. Mr. Train wandered over to the tall windows. Warm sunlight tinted his grayness a faint golden color.

Van said with affected heartiness, "Well, what goes on?"

"I don't know," Train said. "This was McBride's idea."

They both looked at McBride. He felt nervously of the gun in his waistband, thinking he might have lost it. It was still there. He looked at the open wall safe behind the desk. "Well," he said finally, almost regretfully, "it seems that all roads lead to you, William Van."

"All what roads?"

McBride slanted a quick look at Train. The gray man was doing absolutely nothing. McBride hoped he would continue to do nothing. He moistened his lips. "Well," he said, "take Mrs. Carmichael. She is indebted to you for several grand. Did you think she was ever going to pay you?"

Van scowled. "She'd have paid, all right."

"Didn't you think you might somehow be able to incriminate her husband through her? In case things blew up in your face?"

"What things?"

McBride appealed to Mr. Train. "We don't seem to be getting anywhere, do we?"

"Oh, I don't know," Train said. "I'm interested, even if Van isn't. Continue, Mr. McBride."

McBride looked almost as harried as William Van. He said, "Then there's that dancer, Juanita. She worked for Van, remember? Until she was knocked off."

"That rap is your worry," Van said, "not mine." He slopped

some more rye in his glass. Fishy eyes were unpleasantly angry and—McBride hoped—just a trifle apprehensive.

"You remember the guy Swiggart?" McBride asked this of Train, who said he remembered Swiggart very well indeed. "Well, that's another funny thing," McBride said. "Swiggart was quite a frequenter of the Natividad. That's where he met Juanita. A nice place, the Club Natividad. A natural when it comes to contacting workers from the dam. And incidentally, who would be in a better position than the genial host to know who could be bought and who couldn't?"

"I'll bite," Van said. "Who?"

"Nobody."

"Maybe that's who you're looking for," Van said.

McBride ignored this. He kept looking at Train, because he wasn't absolutely sure which way Train would jump. The guy still gave him goose pimples. He said, "After Swiggart was gone I could only locate one other guy who might have been hired to do a little sabotage work on the side. This guy wasn't such a hot bet because he himself had lost an arm. But the minute I started after him he was knocked off. Funny, hunh?"

Train appeared to be looking out the windows. "Who was that?"

"A Mex named Tony Garcia."

Van waved a huge fist at the morning paper. "I just got through reading about it. Number 4 mangled him up something awful."

"But he was dead at the time," McBride said. "He was knifed in the alley back of your place and carted down to the main line later. I rode with him. I ought to know."

Train turned slightly, so that his back was to the light and his face in shadow. "Another of your roads, McBride?"

"A direct road. The hacker Engstrom is known to be associated with me. He went into the Natividad and unbuttoned his lip in the wrong place. By the time I got down there Garcia had got it. He lived long enough to tell me who slit him."

"And who was this?" Train asked gently.

"Van."

The fat man ran a hand over his thinning hair. He was looking, not at McBride, but at Train. "He's lying, boss."

"I talked to Petey, too," McBride said. "And Scarface." He coughed. "This was before I fogged them in the box car."

William Van screamed then, like a horse in a flaming barn, and his hand came away from the back of his neck with a knife in it. The knife caught the light, seeming to hover in midair for seconds before it sang toward the windows. There was a sickening thud as it hit flesh. McBride, tugging at his gun, looked with some surprise at Mr. Train. The haft of the knife was sticking straight out of Train's body, but he paid it no attention whatever. Quite deliberately he took the little gun out of his sleeve and emptied it into William Van. He was rather apologetic about the whole thing.

Van fell as clumsily as a water buffalo. The desk was scarcely big enough to hide his body. McBride ran to Train's side.

"I'll take your arm, please," Train said politely. "An arm to the door, please."

OUT IN the hall there was the pound of running feet. McBride practically carried Train to the door. They got there just as someone put a tentative hand on the knob. "Go away, boys," Train said evenly, distinctly. "We won't be needing you."

The feet went away. McBride said, "Well, blow me down, are they your men or Van's?"

"Van's," Train said. "It just happens that the town is mine." He leaned a little more heavily on McBride. "Van was getting a little too big for Palos Verde, I'm afraid." He reached up and pulled the knife out of his own shoulder. Then he fainted. McBride carried him over to the divan before he went back and saw that the door was securely locked. After a while he called the police.

He was running up quite a phone bill for Van's heirs when Mr. Train spoke from the couch. "You've been a big help to me,

McBride. Without you to stir things up I might not have got to Van before he got to me."

McBride looked at him. "Would you like me to notify your sister?"

"My sister?"

"Lou Queen."

Train said simply:

"Lou Queen is my wife, McBride."

"The hell she is!"

Train smiled. It wasn't a particularly nice smile. "No matter what she is; no matter what I am, nothing can change that. She is still my wife. You see, McBride, in a town noted for divorces, she has never been able to get one. Because I wouldn't let her. Originally that was to punish her. What she is doing now is meant to punish me. Funny, isn't it?" He leaned over and took a handkerchief from William Van's pocket. He pressed the handkerchief against the wound.

McBride said, "She thinks you are responsible for what's been happening around here. She as much as told me so."

Train nodded. "She would like to see me dead, I think."

"But for heaven's sake, why?"

Train shrugged. The movement turned the cloth against his shoulder crimson, but his lips still curved in that whimsical, yet somehow terrible, smile. "Lou ran away from me once, McBride. She would have married him had I given her a divorce. I didn't. By and by he didn't want to marry her any more."

McBride sucked air into his lungs. "And I thought I was a good hater!" He went back to his phoning. After a time, as though he were very tired, he put the phone down and stared at Train. "The man was Leeds?"

"The man was Leeds."

CHAPTER XXII

TO THE BITTER END

"THIS ALWAYS EMBARRASSES me," McBride said. He didn't look embarrassed. He looked haggard. He looked like he had a hangover a yard long. Comparing himself with the rest of them he felt distinctly shabby. On this trip alone his clothes had been scrubbed and pressed so often they looked as though he'd bought them second hand. It was slightly after one in the afternoon, and the management of the Grand National had kindly allowed the meeting to take place in the ladies' lounge, off the main lobby.

Erin Rourke and Franz Charles sat on a love seat, as opposite as the two poles. Rourke, short and chubby and ruddy-faced, looked like a book-maker who liked his liquor. Charles was the austere and dignified statesman. For the hundredth time McBride envied the guy his clothes, or at least his manner of wearing them.

Colin Leeds, over in one corner on a spindly, uncomfortable-looking gilt chair, chewed worriedly on his fingernails. His father was not present. Lou Queen was not there either. Carmichael, of the Five Companies, brooded over something, probably his wife's debts. He seemed to care little whether or not Leeds & Leeds relinquished their contracts.

Miss Ford and Sheila Mason stood by the windows, watching McBride. They had little to say to each other. The gathering was nicely rounded out by Lieutenant Harry Beale, who filled the arch with his sloppy bulk and alternately picked his teeth and examined what his excavations brought to light.

Presently Beale stood aside and allowed Mr. Train to enter. Train was very weak. He leaned rather heavily on his cane and his left sleeve was empty. The bandages gave him a bulky, unnatural look. He sat quietly after a brief nod at everyone.

Volatile Erin Rourke couldn't stand the continued silence. He popped exasperatedly to his feet. "Damn it, what are we waiting for? What's the idea of all this, anyway? You, McBride— you got Van, didn't you?"

"No," McBride said, "Mr. Train got Van. I got the guy Van was working for."

Everybody looked properly stunned at this. Everybody but Sheila Mason. Sheila was competent and slender and trim in tweeds. A small hat, not too ridiculous, went well with her coppery-gold hair. Her fine hands were quiet and composed about her bag. She lifted an eyebrow at McBride and he shook his head slightly, not yet.

Kay Ford, taller than Sheila, smoked nervously. The sun made her dark hair an ebony casque. Her blue eyes were wide, a little mocking. It was interesting, seeing the two women together like that, McBride thought. Interesting and instructive.

He said, "It occurred to me very early in the case that the trouble originated not in Palos Verde, but in Los Angeles. Certain of my predecessors had trouble right from the start; trouble that almost any dick would have been able to avoid if his arrival hadn't been announced in advance. I tried to overcome this handicap by letting it be known I was coming in by train. A man was killed under the misapprehension that he was a guy named Rex McBride. I saw him killed. I think that perhaps this was my main reason for bucking the thing. That job made me pretty sick. I'm still sick about it."

Rourke coughed loudly. "So you quit the Alliance."

"So I quit the Alliance. On the surface, at least. I ostensibly went to work for Carmichael, thinking I could worm my way into his confidence." He looked at Carmichael. "You had the best motive of all, you know."

"Are you accusing me of anything?"

"I don't think so." McBride lit a cigarette nervously. He felt a certain kinship for Miss Ford. "So Mr. Carmichael had the best motive of all for directing, or at least financing the sabotage. His outfit wanted the project in the first place. They would surely get it if Leeds & Leeds failed. They were the only other competent bidders. So we considered Mr. Carmichael. But there were other possible motives. At least two of them. One was revenge against one or the other—or both—of the two Leeds. Through inadvertence the senior Mr. Leeds let me know that he hated St. George Train. I thought it quite possible that this hatred was reciprocated. As it has turned out I now know this to be a fact. Mr. Train did and still does hate Mr. Leeds. We needn't go into the cause.

"The third motive was profit through indirection. By forcing Leeds & Leeds stock down, by knowing in advance that it was going down, a smart operator could make himself a pot of money. Strangely enough, I discovered that this motive also fit our Mr. Train. Outside of Mr. Carmichael, Mr. Train was our best prospect. He owned the town." McBride paused briefly to stare malevolently at the gross Harry Beale. "He even owned the police force."

Colin Leeds stood up violently. "Get on with it, McBride! Do we have to listen to your life history?"

McBride's eyes smoldered. The way he felt he would have been glad to take on the whole lot of them in a knock-down-drag-out fist fight. "I'm merely trying to make you see that I've been working. Maybe some one of you will be appreciative enough to see that I get paid. I've been pushed around by damned near everybody in this lousy town; I've been shot at— yes, and hit, too; I've had my feet burned off me. I have, in fact, become very sick of the sight of all of you and if you don't like it you know what you can do!"

Franz Charles was sympathetic in an elegant, remote way. "I'll see that you're paid, McBride. No one doubts you've earned a fee."

"THANKS," McBride said. He took a deep breath. "Unfortunately I became a little too involved in personal feuds to get the proper perspective on the vastness of the project itself. I did, however, understand what it meant to snuff out the lives of fourteen men all at once. I have been very eager indeed to find the guy who was responsible. Not William Van, except that he might lead me to the guy behind him.

"Van was a tool, a rather sharp tool with an idea he could run Palos Verde if there were no Mr. Train. Van and his employer probably conceived the idea of foisting credit for the sabotage on either Train or Carmichael."

Sheila was looking at him strangely. "But Rex—"

He smiled at her. "I know what I'm doing, hon." He frowned, recalling his last words. "Van had the opportunity and the will. He didn't have the capital. As usual in a case like that it is the guy with the money who is boss. Van was the killer, the procurer of all the other killers. The boss made his killings in the market. He probably never had a gun in his hand but he's going to hang as sure as God made little apples."

Sheila said, "But Rex, I thought you said Train shot Van. If he never had a gun in his hand—"

"The guy isn't Train. It's perfectly true that Train refused to okay a loan to Leeds & Leeds. He guessed the trend of the market and made money off it. He didn't force the stock down." He made a bitter mouth. "I'm a hell of a detective. Train himself had to point out that the guy who sold short *before* the first accident was probably the guy I was after."

"But it *was* Train. I told you—"

"I know you did, hon," he said gently. "And you lied."

She flinched as though he had struck her. "Rex, you can't know what you're saying!"

Colin Leeds got out of his chair. "See here, McBride, Miss

Mason is on our legal staff. Why, she's practically my father's right hand."

"She's also a woman," McBride said heavily. "A woman I'd have given my right arm to marry. It just happens she didn't care for my style, or the way I don't accumulate money. She prefers Mr. Charles."

Things were a little upset for a moment. Harry Beale finally stopped picking his teeth and hauled out his gun. He menaced everyone impartially. "Shut up and sit down!"

They all sat down. Franz Charles was the most composed of any in the room. He favored McBride with a bleak smile. "This is a very serious business, McBride."

"You're telling me!" McBride didn't look at Sheila. He thought, If I look at her now I'll go out and shoot myself later. He looked at the impassive Train instead. "You know what we found in William Van's safe."

Train nodded. He stared without visible emotion at Charles. "This is my town, Mr. Charles. You and Van very nearly wrecked it." He sighed. "Often it seems strange to me that a man of your caliber should have so little sense. You might have known that Van would try to protect himself; that a hold over you would be pretty good insurance against the future. We found records to prove the connection between you. You needn't have worried so about the bills McBride had. True, they could be traced back to you and they would bear—we think—your fingerprints. But there were other things you overlooked, because you thought that Van had overlooked them. Van was gross. He was a coward. But he wasn't dumb."

Charles seemed to shrink in upon himself. He looked desperately to Sheila for help. She quietly fainted. He wet his lips. "I—I don't quite understand, McBride. I thought Sheila—your trust in her integrity would—"

"Once," McBride said in a curiously reminiscent voice, "I gave a little girl some flowers. She remembered them, and me, even though I was a heel to her. She knew Miss Mason. She

knew what Miss Mason meant to me. And so, when you flew
up to Los Angeles last night and Miss Mason met you to save
time, this little girl recognized her. And you very nearly killed
her. Perhaps you thought you had, I don't know." He got up,
more tired than he had ever been in his life. "I talked with the
little girl this morning. I checked all the stock angles by phone
through the Los Angeles police department. When Miss
Mason's story didn't coincide I knew how it was."

FRANZ CHARLES got to his feet too, and they stood there
facing each other. Charles' face was even grayer now than Train's.
"But you must have had some inkling before—"

"Not of Sheila and you," McBride said. "Of you alone, yes.
The stock motive fitted you as well as it did Erin Rourke, whom
I once suspected. You were an officer of an insurance company,
but like most of us your personal ambitions were higher than
your job. I remembered that you passed through the lobby at
the moment I was paying Train. You could have thought the
two bills were the ones you wanted." His sudden laugh was
brittle, without humor. "It occurred to me that the *Do Not
Disturb* tag on your room signal could easily mean that you
weren't in the room. I wondered where else you could be. This
morning, while we waited up at William Van's, Mr. Train helped
me locate your pilot."

Charles decided quite suddenly to run. He was almost to the
windows when Harry Beale shot him. McBride went past Beale,
out into the lobby. He didn't care whether Franz Charles was
alive or dead. All he wanted to do was get away, so that he would
not have to see Sheila again, ever.

Miss Ford touched his arm. "What do you get out of all this,
Rex?"

He looked at her. Presently he smiled. "If I'm lucky," he said,
"I may get you. I'll probably have to watch you every minute,
but at least I'll know exactly where I stand."

Miss Ford took his arm then, and helped him across the
lobby. "You'll never know, Rex," she said. "You'll never even
guess." And there were real tears in her fine blue eyes.

ABOUT THE AUTHOR

Cleve Adams occupies a prominent place as a writer of "realistic" detective fiction, a member of the so-called "hard-boiled" school of which Dashiell Hammett was the founder. Mr. Adams' books include "The Black Door," "And Sudden Death," "Decoy," and "Sabotage," all published by Dutton.

I HAVE BEEN writing for some eight or ten years. Prior to becoming a writer, I was many, many things. Out of a vast variety of experiences I probably accumulated an understanding of human nature and its motivations. And there, in a nutshell, is the reason for what small success I have had as a writer. Neither consciously nor unconsciously have I ever permitted one of my characters to do a single thing which did not have a *logical, airtight motive:* a motive completely understandable to anyone. You will never find, for example, a character of mine jumping out of a second-story window when he could just as well walk down the stairs. On the other hand, if the stairs are blocked, or there are seven guys waiting out there to demolish our hero, then he has a perfectly good motive for using the window.

I use this sound motivation technique in even the little things. How much more important is it, then, to seat the story itself on a firm foundation! Why search around for obscure motives, or tricky motives, or downright silly motives, when the good, old-fashioned solid kind are right there before you? Why don't more writers ask themselves, "Well, what would I myself do in a given situation?" And then have the character do likewise!

With regard to weaving plausible yarns, if mine are plausible, analysis will show that said plausibility stems directly from this urge of mine to have my *characters* act like *people*. Maybe you, personally, don't know that kind of people; maybe their foibles and peculiarities are *exaggerated;* but *conceivably,* if placed in his or her position, you yourself would be very apt to act as he or she did.

As to creating suspense, well, just for fun let's take my star detective, Rex McBride, for an example. Here is a guy who is a heel in many ways. Yet he has a good point here and there. He loves and hates, lies and cheats, gets drunk and has a hangover, even as you and I. If someone kicks him in the stomach, it *hurts.* It hurts like nobody's business! And if someone does him an injury, he doesn't say, "That's okay, pal, I forgive you." You're darned right he doesn't. He gets sore about it, the same as anyone else in this day and age. But he doesn't just hate a man because that man has a crooked nose, or eats with his knife! He has a real, a *very* real, motive for doing the things he does. Lord, there we are, back to MOTIVE again! Well, can I help it? It's the MOTIVE that makes him do the things that create the SUSPENSE.

Let's analyze that: McBride is a private detective. He is hired to do a certain job. Now if there is one single thing about McBride that is admirable, it is his singleness of purpose. Maybe there is a point of honor involved; maybe his pride, his ego, or his reputation for getting results are responsible for the *drive* which forces him, and the reader, on. He has been hired to do a job and he's going to do it. Come hell or high water, he's going to do it.

And naturally, in a story, the "Hell and high water," or some very evil-minded guys and gals, are in there trying to stop him from accomplishing his purpose. The point is, they're in there *trying,* every minute, every page, just as hard as "McBride" himself is *trying.* He wants something. He wants it more than he wants anything in the world. And his antagonists are just as fiercely determined that he shan't have it. Why? Because they want to keep it themselves. Or they don't want to be hanged by the neck until they are dead. Or something. Ergo, if we don't have SUSPENSE now, we have a very reasonable facsimile.

Our hero is *always,* up to the very end, in *imminent danger* of *losing,* if not his life, at least that thing which he *prizes,* or is *trying desperately to get.*

As I see it, suspense is built on MENACE. This urgency both for and against, does not only apply to a detective-mystery story. What matter if it be only a golf tournament? Our hero wants to win, doesn't he? And our villain, or villainess, simply isn't going to stand for his winning. No, sir! He wants to win, too. He wants to win, even if he has to resort to unsportsman-like shenanigans, by golly. So is he a menace? You bet your sweet life he is. And does the *struggle* between the two opposing forces create SUSPENSE? Well, if the writer has done his job, it should.

Of course everybody knows all this. Every writers' magazine, every textbook on the subject of writing, is loaded down with it. But somehow, as it was in my own case, the necessary emphasis isn't there. That is all I hope to do, to emphasize this for others.

And while we're on *that* subject, my article is not going to work the same for everybody. I've tried it out on other professionals; on the novices who sometimes come to me for advice and criticism; yes, even on my own son, who may some day yet become a writer. And offhand I'd say that perhaps ten per cent are affected as I was. But, in this business, if you can help even ten per cent of your fellow travelers you aren't doing so badly.

Now for some other angles on the way I work. There has been an awful lot written about PLOT. Well, certainly a plot is necessary, unless you write for *Harper's, The Atlantic,* or maybe *The New Yorker.* So what is a plot? Essentially, a plot may be fully and adequately described, as it has been, in that old chestnut: "Get your hero into trouble; get him out of it."

The main thing that is lacking there is that it doesn't mention *why* your hero gets into trouble. To me that is the vital essence of the whole thing. He gets into trouble *because* he is trying to do a certain thing. If I may say so, a *very* certain thing, and a thing that the normal, every-day human being (the reader) can easily and thoroughly understand without a diagram.

And the *trouble* develops *because* someone, or a whole flock of someones, or maybe the elements, are doing their damnedest to keep our hero from his goal.

Well! In the generally accepted sense I myself do not plot. By that I mean that I do not sit down and work out a detailed, blow-by-blow synopsis. I know many writers who do. I know many writers who, by the same token, rewrite their stories three and four times before the finished script goes out. And of these writers I know but one or two whose finished work, perfect in every last *technical* detail, has in it one single spark of life or real characterization. In other words, everything is there that the textbooks say ought to be there, but the stuff is as wooden and flavorless as some of the breakfast food you eat.

So what do I do? Well, first I get a character. I get a man that walks around, and breathes, and sometimes even spits on the carpet if he happens to feel like it. Sure, I romanticize him! I make him the kind of fellow I secretly would like to be; I make him do the things I'd like to do, if I had spunk enough, or were smart enough. And next I find him something terribly important to accomplish; at least it's terribly important to *him*, once he gets started. And then, being a craftsman of sorts, I know I've got to get some other real red-blooded people, either to help him or hinder him. So I do that.

Well, the first thing you know, things pile up until the poor guy is in one terrific jam. Rarely do I bother with how I'm going to get him out—not at first. I'm too busy getting him in, and sweating with him, and getting kicked in the teeth. Then, along about the middle of the job—be it slick, pulp, or book—I go back and try to figure out *why* everybody did what he did. Sometimes this is pretty difficult. That is really when I start plotting. But believe me, if I can't find a good *logical* motive for each and every part, out that part comes.

I hope Albert Richard Wetjen will forgive me for this: It came to me second-hand from a mutual friend, as many of his words of wisdom have come: "The pulp story is concerned with WHAT and HOW. The slick is concerned with WHY."

It is my contention that even the much-maligned pulp need not be *only* concerned with WHAT and HOW. The more of the WHY you can get into *any* story, pulp, slick, or literary, the better story it will be, and the better writer you will be, and if you want seriously to go on up—as most of us do—you will not say to yourself, "Nuts, this is meant for Terrible Tales, why bother!" You'll give a great deal of thought to the WHY, and keep putting it in there, even for Terrible Tales, and some day somebody is going to "discover" you, and lift you right out of that hole, same as they did C.S. Forester and his Captain Hornblower.

Coming Next Week

SABOTAGE

A Brilliant New Novel by
CLEVE F. ADAMS

The strength of the nation was dedicated to building the great dam at Palos Verde, and when a sinister foeman determined to sabotage that life-giving project, it fell to the lot of Rex McBride, the world's most unorthodox detective, to attempt a job at which the government's daring, well-trained operatives shied.

DIAMONDS NORTH

An Exciting Novelette by
BAYNARD KENDRICK

Stan Rice rode the Limited as it thundered through the southern night, and the clack of each rail-joint, he knew, warned of murder to come. . . .

THE CLUE OF THE SKELETON'S FINGER

An Unusual Novelette by
WILLIAM BRANDON

Death bore in its bony hand a note which only the lifeless could read, and on that grim island off the Georgia coast, Sam Ireland came face to face with the restless ghost from an empty tomb. . . .

Shorter fiction by Edward A. Dieckmann,
E. O. Umsted, James Holden, Lawrence Treat &
Richard Sale

Detective Fiction Weekly